OUT OF THE COCOON

Gilbert Depretto

OUT OF THE COCOON

Gil Desbiens

Out of the Cocoon by Gil Desbien
Out of the Cocoon © 2004 Gil Desbien

Publisher's note: This book is a work of fiction. Names, characters, places and incidents are the product of the author's imagination or are used fictitiously, and any resemblance to actual persons living or dead, events or locales is entirely coincidental.

Manufactured in Canada.

Library and Archives Canada Cataloguing in Publication

Desbiens, Gil, 1925-
        Out of the cocoon / Gil Desbiens.

Also available in electronic format.
ISBN 1-897098-41-3

        I Title.

PS8607.E76O98 2004   C813'.6   C2004-903678-5

TreeSide Press
905 Fort Street.
Victoria, BC, Canada V8V 3K3
http://www.treesidepress.ca

DEDICATION

This book is dedicated to two very good friends: Adell Martin, whose persistence kept me writing, and Myrle McLeod for her editing and overall efforts get the book published.

CHAPTER I

Joe Martel, crawling along the limb of the tree, had barely cleared the top wire of the fence when a rifle shot cracked through the air. I was about thirty feet away when Martel hit the ground. I threw myself face down in the tall weeds to hide, sure that he had been shot and was lying dead a few feet from the fence. Was there something I could do to help him? Carefully raising my head, I saw the watchman running toward a building a few hundred feet away, then Joe flew by me at a full run, yelling, "Hurry! Get in the car."

"Have you been shot?" I asked. "No," he gasped, "just shot at. But I think I ripped my pants."

By the time I reached the car, Joe was fiddling with something under the dashboard. My heart was pounding and I wanted out of there as soon as possible. "Why can't you get it started?" I demanded as I jumped into the front seat and slammed the door.

"Haven't got the keys," he admitted. That's when I realized he had stolen the car.

After what seemed like an eternity, the motor roared and he put it in gear, leaving a cloud of dust behind. When we came to the highway, he made a sharp right turn and I swore we were going to flip over. We sailed past the mine and through Kearns at more than sixty miles per hour, neither of us saying anything. But I was thinking plenty.

I was thinking that the farm looked pretty good right now, school looked good, even trapping with my dad in −50F seemed like a reasonable occupation. I remembered that first year he took me with him.

It was 1935 and I was nine years old. School was out, summer had arrived and it had been terrific so far. Every day the sun shone in a clear blue sky with just a sprinkle of rain now and then. The farmers, of course, would have liked to see more rain in the spring, but now hoped the dry weather would remain until the hay crop was safely in the barn.

Sometimes my mother would say we were having a nice summer to make up for the long, grueling winter, with record cold and winds of forty miles per hour blowing the snow into drifts of ten to twelve feet high. I heard her complain more than once about the severe winters and the accompanying misery.

"It's not enough that we are poor and dressed in rags and the country is in a deep depression," she would say. "It seems that the weather is against us as well. I wonder what affliction we are going to be struck with next?"

But I didn't worry much about the future. The present was all that was important to me and I just wanted to have some fun for the next two months. I had passed my exams easily and was looking forward to beginning Grade IV in the fall. I had done well in multiplications and was anxious to learn divisions. After watching a pal who was in Grade IV do his homework, I knew I wasn't going to have any trouble. How surprised my teacher was going to be with what I had learned!

There wasn't much free time on the farm; there were always chores to be done and Mom saw to it that work came before play. The chore I hated the most was carrying water from the river every morning for the garden. There were other jobs I didn't mind doing but I wasn't given a choice.

Mother was barely five feet tall, had a husky build and could move quickly. She was a hard worker herself with a will of iron, and spoke with the voice of authority.

My brother Paul was the eldest in the family. He was thirteen, slim and tall, and he walked with a bit of a bounce. Paul liked to boast about his accomplishments.

Then came Gemma who would be twelve in January. She was stout and bubbly, always coming up with something to make us laugh. I was next to Gemma and four years younger than Paul. Like him, I was tall, but much slimmer, shy and more reserved. I was going to be ten on the first of October and Paul fourteen on the twelfth of the same month. My sister Noella was six, and having been born two months premature, she was frail and sickly. Donat was two and the new baby, Roland, was two months old. The last two in the family had blue eyes. My mother said it was because they were born during the blueberry season.

Dad, who had been working away from home for most of the winter, was back on the farm that summer. Unable to find a job, he was busy mending fences and doing repairs to the buildings that had been badly neglected by the previous tenant. Unfortunately, this big beautiful farm didn't belong to us. The town's priest, who was always praising Dad for doing such a good job maintaining it, owned it.

Dad wasn't happy working on the farm; he was always complaining about one thing or another: blaming the government for the depression and for keeping men working at starvation wages. I guess he really wanted to have a farm of his own where his work would amount to something over the years.

Once in a while Dad would go to town to talk to people he knew in order to keep abreast of things and to find out about any new development that might take place. Late one afternoon he came home very excited. He said he had met Mr. Magee, a man he had worked with at Quebec Fishery. Dad said that Mr. Magee knew of a company that had been awarded a road contract beginning a few miles from Senneterre, to service the mines in the Chibogamou area.

The company had established its office at Cedar Rapids, about thirty-five miles from Senneterre, and as soon as Mr. Magee could get away he was going to see if he could land a subcontract from them. If he did, he wanted Dad to go in as a partner.

Some time later Mr. Magee came over to tell us he had landed a contract with the company to dig two miles of ditches, and there was a camp ready to move in that would accommodate as many as eight men. Paul's education ended at that point. He went to camp with Dad to begin the life of a labourer.

That fall I went back to school and was happy to have Sister Cecile as my teacher again. She had been my teacher the previous year and I liked her. I think she liked me, too, because she was often at my desk helping me with one subject or another. She either liked me or else I was very dumb and I prefer to think she liked me.

The second week of November Dad came home for an overnight stay. We were all happy to see him and asked a lot of questions but he wasn't very talkative and neither was Mom. We had a late dinner and to our disappointment, Mom sent us all to bed very early that evening. From where I was sleeping in the attic of the old farmhouse, I could hear them arguing for a long time, although I couldn't make out the words. I thought it was because Mom didn't want Dad to be so far away from us that winter, but I found out the real reason the next morning.

It was a Monday morning. Gemma was sitting at the table next to Dad, who was smoking his pipe and drinking a cup of tea. Mom was at the stove and no one was saying a word. I took a seat at the end of the table, facing Dad, and listened to Gemma trying to make conversation with him, with little success.

Finally Mom sat down and in a low voice she announced the bad news to me in as gentle a way as she could. "I made only one school lunch this morning," she said. Then, she added, "I don't need to make one for you any more because you are going to camp with your dad."

She went on to say that they needed a good man like me in camp to keep the fire going in the stove so the food wouldn't freeze, and perhaps to peel a few potatoes for the men.

Dad perked up and added, "And set some rabbit snares to help put food on the table."

Mid-morning found the two of us standing on the dock in freezing weather waiting for the tugboat to take us to Cedar Rapids.

I was hanging on to a feed bag containing a change of clothes for myself and thinking that I'd rather be in school sitting behind my desk. Finally the tugboat arrived and we boarded. Dad led the way down below near the engine where there was a bench. We sat down and after what seemed a long time the engine roared to life and I heard the skipper yell, "Cast off!"

The roar of the engine was deafening and the smell of diesel fuel was just as bad. I could see through the small porthole that the boat was moving, leaving the dock and going down the Bell River, heading north across Lake Parent, taking the Bell River again at the end of the lake.

I had been hungry for a long time when I saw Dad opening a brown paper bag and taking out a loaf of bread and a large wedge of cheese. He said to me, "You had better eat good now because this is our supper."

I ate as much as I could, washing it down with a cup of ice cold water from the river.

It was dark by the time we arrived at Cedar Rapids, which was where the head office was located. It was also the depot for supplies for the contractors. It felt good to get on the dock to stretch my legs and to get away from the unvented cabin that was filled with the stinking smell of diesel fuel and burning motor oil.

We made our way to a shed-like building where we soon found the office. I waited outside while Dad went in to do whatever business was necessary. A few minutes later he came out and led the way to a group of huge tents, three of them side by side. Dad explained that those were bunkhouses and we were going to sleep in the middle one.

We made our way into the tent. It was very dark and we had to go by feel to find the pallets that were scattered on the ground. I took one and Dad took the next. I put my bag down and began making my bed with the bedding provided. I was tired after the long journey and I really didn't care what my bed was like as long as I had a place to sleep. I lay down and covered myself, but the smell of mold and filth from the blankets kept me awake for a long time.

It was dark when Dad woke me up. I thought it was still the middle of the night, but I was well rested. The first thing Dad said was, "Don't look for a place to wash; there isn't one. We'll go eat the way we are."

The cookhouse was a long tent with board walls and floor and there were four long tables where a few men were already seated, waiting for the food to be served. We sat at a table with three men who appeared to be afraid to talk. After a short while a man appeared from behind a door that must have led into the kitchen. He was wearing a dirty white apron and pants that needed a good wash, too, which made me wonder about the last time he'd had a bath. He was carrying a large pot of pork and beans that he placed in the middle of the table. It seemed that every man there was trying to get to the pot at the same time. Dad and I were the last ones to fill our plates. I watched some of the men pouring blackstrap molasses over their beans and then taking huge pieces of bread and soaking the bread in the molasses. They devoured their food as if they hadn't eaten in months.

The cook might not have had a bath for months, but the beans were delicious. I took a second helping.

Dad wasn't one to waste time and I had barely finished my tea when he said, "Well, man, we'd better get underway. The first thirty-five miles was easy, but we have to walk the second and we have to get there tonight."

I grabbed my bag that I kept by my side so it wouldn't get stolen, and began following Dad along the trail in the darkness. It was just breaking daylight when snow began to fall to add to the six or seven inches that were already on the ground.

Dad was walking pretty fast, never looking back to see how far behind I was. That worried me a bit. For the best part of the morning I kept close to him, though the trail was narrow and we sometimes encountered high mounds of moss that made walking more difficult. Once in a while I could hear Dad talking to himself but I could never make out what he was saying.

At about mid-morning I began to tire and Dad must have sensed it because we stopped for a few moments. He insisted I give him my bag, which he fitted to the top of his packsack that already looked pretty heavy to me. We started out again with him saying, "Don't give up on me now; we still have a long way to go."

Once I clearly heard Dad say, "I wish this snow would stop, at least until we get to camp. Please, good Lord, give us a break."

The snow was starting to build up on the trail. Then Dad said the words I had been waiting to hear. "Do you see that big spruce tree over there?" It was about a half a mile ahead.

I said, "Yes, I can see it."

"Well," he said, "we are going to stop there and have some lunch. I bet you could eat a big platter of pork and beans about now."

We both got under the boughs of the tree to shelter ourselves from the snow. I found a piece of broken timber to sit on but Dad ate his lunch standing up, as I would see him do many times later on when we worked the trap line. We didn't have pork and beans, but Dad opened the same brown paper bag from the previous day and we finished off the bread and cheese, washing it down with a handful of snow.

We spent only a few minutes eating lunch before Dad loaded his pipe and we took to the trail again, with the snow falling heavier than before. That must have worried Dad a little because he increased the pace and I nearly had to run to keep up.

At that time of year there were only about five hours of daylight, so we ended up walking a long time in total darkness. I was getting tired, and I was hungry—again—when Dad finally said, "I think I can see the camp light ahead of us. I sure hope I'm right." He was right, because a little farther on I could see the light myself and felt a sense of relief.

As we came in the door we saw five men sitting at the table near the kerosene lamp that was positioned atop a zinc bucket to give more light. The men jumped to their feet to greet us. One of them, whose name I later learned was Roland, asked before we had time to sit down, "Are you hungry?"

Dad said, "Yes, we're starving." Roland went to the stove and came back with a large pot of stew that he placed on the table. We each grabbed a plate and filled it.

After eating such a big meal I felt so tired and sleepy that I could barely move. Dad caught me nodding at the table and promptly showed me to my bed that was already made and waiting for me. I took the time to wash, got undressed, and jumped into bed. I drifted off to sleep almost immediately.

I was the last one to get up in the morning. I noticed Roland was at the stove cooking hot cakes—and lots of them. I hurried to get cleaned up and took my place at the table. While I was eating breakfast Dad explained what my duties were going to be. I was to wash the breakfast dishes after the men made their lunches and went to work. Then I would dry the dishes and put them away, keep a low-burning fire in the stove, and keep the wood box full at all times.

Then I could go out and cut some firewood, if I felt like it, but I didn't have to. At four o'clock I was to peel a large pot full of potatoes, cook them for twenty minutes and keep them warm in the oven until the men came in from work. At that time one of them would take over and cook the rest of the meal.

My first day went by quickly. I made everyone's bed and after sweeping the floor I found time to try my hand at sawing firewood. Having a clean floor made a big hit with the men when they came in that night.

I soon got used to my routine. The work wasn't hard but it kept me busy so I didn't have time to get lonely. Mother had packed some of my books and writing paper but I didn't have much time to study except on Sundays when either Roland or René, Mr. Magee's son who was about a year older than Paul, helped me with some of my studies. During the week I'd do all the indoor chores, then I'd make the round of my rabbit snares so I had no time left to do any school work. The crew came from work long after dark and everyone went to bed shortly after supper.

Christmas and New Year's Day came and went and the snow kept falling. There was a lot of it on the ground and the weather was bitterly cold every single day. I carried on my same routine day in and day out; then one day something happened that made all the men in camp a bit nervous.

It was February and the mailman, who made his round every two weeks, didn't show up on time to deliver the mail, take the food order, or deliver the previous week's order. My dad and Mr. Magee decided to send a volunteer to Cedar Rapids to find out what had happened. Roland volunteered to go and left long before daylight the next day. He promised to return as soon as possible, but it was three days before he got back with the bad news. The company had gone into receivership. Bouchard et Rouleau, who had posted no bond for the contract, was now bankrupt. This was very discouraging news for a group of men who had worked so hard for more than three months–all for nothing!

It must have been well after midnight when I went to bed while the rest of the men sat at the table trying to make a decision on what to do. When I got up the next morning I heard the verdict: the only sensible decision was to spend this last day in camp, gather the tools from the job, get our clothes packed and hit the trail as early as possible the next morning. Dad was confident we could make it to Cedar Rapids in one day if we all took turns at breaking the trail.

Dad came with me to raise my rabbit snares and he spent the rest of the day like the other men, packing his belongings and cleaning the camp in order to leave it in good order.

It was 3:30 a.m. the next day when we got on the trail. I was packing a fair load, but luckily I was the last one in the line, which gave me the advantage of a well-opened trail. I was carrying a pocket full of cookies as well, in case I got hungry.

We got to Cedar Rapids long after dark. We all went into the one tent to sleep, without even asking permission. The next morning Dad and Mr. Magee went to the cookhouse, which was still open, to ask about getting some breakfast. However, the cook told them that if he got caught serving a meal to someone without a ticket he would be fired and he couldn't afford to risk his job. None of the men had thirty-five cents to buy a ticket, so none of us had any breakfast. Dad later went back to plead with the cook, telling him we had thirty-five miles to walk and we just *had* to have something to eat for the trip. The cook gave Dad a bag full of cookies and cautioned him not to mention a word of it to anyone.

For the first nine or ten miles the road was open in order to service the next camp that was in the process of closing down. We made good time walking those few miles but slowed down again at the end of it.

We had picked up five more men who had decided to walk to Senneterre with us and one of them had walked the road on his way to camp. He said there was a cache a few miles farther and we might be able to spend the night there if we had to. We got to the cache after dark. The only thing stored there were hay bales and barrels of diesel fuel–no food at all. Two of the men found some axes, cut off the top of a barrel and set fire to the fuel in order to keep us warm during the night.

Dad tore several bales of hay apart and made a bed for the two of us and I soon went to sleep, but not for long. I guess Dad was afraid I wouldn't make it the rest of the way to town because he woke me up, saying we should get a head start on the men in case I needed to rest. That way we could rest and still get to town the same day, saving us the hardship of sleeping in the snow somewhere along the road.

Dad had cheated on the rest of the men a little. He had hidden some cookies in his pocket and he gave me three of them as we got ready to go. While I was standing by the door eating my cookies, a young native woman wearing a long blue dress went by us with a baby wrapped in her coat. Dad said to me, "She came in last night before I went to sleep and she wasn't carrying a baby then. She slept in the far corner of the cache." We watched her heading north in the deep snow. We never saw her again.

We got on the trail with Dad carrying my packsack and his own. He was breaking the trail as well. Although the weather was very cold, it wasn't long before Dad was covered with perspiration. But he kept plodding forward.

We must have walked for at least six or seven miles, breaking three or four feet of powdered snow. Finally, dead tired and hungry, Dad said to me, "I think we are coming to civilization. I believe I can see smoke coming out of a chimney up ahead." Sure enough, after walking for another quarter of a mile we could see a house and an open winter road a short distance ahead of us. I could see the look of relief on Dad's face. We rested for a few minutes, looking back to see if any of the men were in sight, but we couldn't see anyone. We walked for only a short distance on the open road before coming to the entrance of a farm. Dad led the way to the front door and after a light knock a man opened the door and asked us to come in. Dad told him we had walked all the way from Cedar Rapids and we were very hungry. The man apologized that his wife had gone to town but he would fix us something to eat. He took out a nice pork roast and warmed some potatoes and soon we were sitting at the table filling our empty stomachs. Dad thanked the man and we left.

As we got on the road we could see the rest of the men about a half a mile away. Then we saw a farmer coming out of his road with a team of horses. Dad asked him if he would give us a ride to town and could we wait for the men who were behind us. The man agreed, and as soon as the men arrived we all got onto the sleigh and rode the rest of the way in style, arriving in Senneterre just as darkness was descending.

Once in town we had only to cross the river to get home, less than a mile away. That was the easiest part of the journey.

Mom wasn't surprised to see us. She had heard the company had gone bankrupt and was wondering when we would get home. She was going to fix us something to eat, but Paul was the only one who was hungry. She began to fix him a meal and make a pot of tea for Dad, but I went to bed. I was tired and disgusted. I didn't want to hear any more about Cedar Rapids or any other road-building job. I tried to stay awake by keeping my mind busy thinking of getting back to school, but I drifted off to sleep. I woke up to the noise of brothers and sisters talking loudly and making a racket downstairs, so I got up and joined the rest of the family in the kitchen.

On the Monday following our arrival Mom took me to school and had a long talk with Sister Superior about getting me back into class, but the Sister was adamant. I had been away too long, she said. It would be impossible for me to catch up with the other students. I would have to wait until next fall. Mom and I were both disappointed, but there was nothing we could do.

Shortly before Dad went to Cedar Rapids to work, he had heard the government had opened a new farming area about seven miles from town where ten-acre farms were going for ten dollars. Dad decided to have a look at the area. He liked what he saw so he went to the land office see if it was true that they were selling the farm sites for ten dollars. It was indeed true, so Dad went back and claimed what he thought was the best farm available. There was no road to it yet, but the land agent told him that construction of a road should get under way late in the fall. However, we could try moving there by way of the lake if we didn't want to wait for the road.

Dad didn't want to wait. He planned to build a log house for us on our new property as soon as the hay crop was in the barn that fall. Naturally, Paul and I were anxious to move to the new farm, too. We were imagining all kinds of adventures we would have. The forest would be ours to explore and we would take a lot more interest in working our own land. No more tenant farming!

I was too young to understand why Mother was so reluctant to move away from the priest's farm. We had moved there as a shelter from the depression, "a place to weather the storm," she had once said. She still remembered Dad returning from a job he had worked at for four months without receiving a cent in wages.

Dad had moved our family to Senneterre, where Quebec Fisheries had established its headquarters. The newly-formed company was going to employ men to fish for sturgeon on Notaway Lake near James Bay. Dad got a job as a boatman and net mender. He was not only qualified for those jobs, but was also an experienced sturgeon fisherman. A crew of about thirty men began to move the boats down the Bell River where they encountered rapids and waterfalls every few miles. They had to build pole tracks to move the boats overland to the lower end of the rapids.

Although the plane took a one-ton load of fish to the markets almost every day, after four months the company declared bankruptcy and the crew returned home without any wages. The men were very angry with the company and despaired of being able to feed their families during the long, cold winter ahead.

The Quebec Fisheries' plane had been left tied up at the dock on the river, seemingly forgotten by the bankrupt company. Some of the crew began a vigil on the plane, deciding to hold it at the dock until all the wages were paid. They armed themselves with shotguns and rifles and began a round-the-clock watch.

When word came that the owner of the company was to arrive in Senneterre by train to retrieve the plane, the crew went to the station to meet him face to face. To their dismay, they were met by a small army of RCMP officers who disarmed them and sent them home. The owner was allowed to fly his plane to New York.

Fortunately, luck was with Dad, as it often was. Shortly after his return he heard that the priest was looking for a new tenant for his farm. Dad applied and got it.

Mother remembered these things and it scared her to think of leaving the priest's farm where we had plenty to eat without having to go to the store for everything. But at the same time she felt a sense of adventure and caught the pioneering spirit. She knew deep inside that Dad was not a farmer, but she clung to the hope that maybe one day he might change. It had taken Dad a long time to convince her that he could earn some real money by trapping, where he would be sure of getting the money he worked for– money that was so badly needed to buy clothes and other necessities. After discussing the pros and cons with Dad, she consented to leave our safe haven and start a new life in a world unfamiliar to her.

Dad told the priest we would be leaving in the fall and he wished us well. He gave us a young bull we had raised and told Dad to take all the hay we would need to feed it through the winter. He assured Dad that a well-trained ox would come in very handy to clear the land and do other chores that couldn't be done by hand. As a calf, the bull was so scrawny no one wanted to buy him, and that's why we raised him.

Dad didn't waste any time. He made a harness for the bull and began breaking him. It wasn't an easy task. That bull was a rebel and a fighter! He had been barely one year old when he began jumping the fence to fight the breeding bull in the next pasture, and with his mean disposition he was very hard to handle. We had named him Bully, a name he well deserved.

One day Dad latched Bully to the big white horse and harnessed both of them to the plow. Then the fun began. Bully didn't stand still for long. He leaped high into the air and took off, dragging the big white horse, the plow, and Dad. But after racing for a few yards, Dad regained control and dug the plow deep into the ground to slow the runaway team.

It took a lot of patience and a few bad tumbles, but eventually Dad won the battle. After being harnessed a few times, Bully accepted the fact that he wasn't going to win. He quieted down and became a real pet.

We had just started to mow the hay one afternoon when the new tenant came and introduced himself. He asked if he could take over the milking and the barn chores immediately, as he had six kids and they had nothing to eat in the house. Dad told him he was welcome to do so and could also help himself to the eggs in the chicken coop and some of the vegetables that were ready in the garden.

This arrangement really pleased Dad. He said, more to himself than to any of us, "That's just what I needed; the good Lord is giving me a break. Now we can work longer hours in the field and be able to leave for the new farm a lot sooner than I expected."

That day we worked until dark. Mom brought us a snack late in the afternoon and we sat on the hay listening to Dad telling Mom all about the new farm. We didn't mind working late because haying time was always fun for kids. Gemma and I worked on the wagon placing the hay along the edges of the big rack so we could put on a bigger load. Then we tramped it down by jumping on the hay. Gemma was a pretty hefty girl and Dad would tease her by saying that with all the weight she carried she could make this her career and would be in great demand every summer at haying time. That was Dad's way of kidding with us and Gemma didn't seem to mind, but I never liked it.

The weather stayed good for the ten days it took to get the harvest in. That year there was more hay than we needed to feed the ten cows and a team of horses. The loft was full and there was a huge stack near the barn. We wouldn't have to buy hay for Bully for a long time.

Dad and Paul began getting together the supplies we would need, visiting friends and neighbours to borrow some of the tools necessary to build a log house. Fall came early in the northern part of Quebec; it wasn't unusual to get some heavy frosts or even snow in early October and Dad wanted to have the log house finished and the family moved in long before then.

One of the jobs Dad gave me while he and Paul were making their preparations was to bundle some hay to take with us to feed Bully. Dad showed me what size to make the bundles and how to tie them with binder twine. I was to make at least two hundred–three bundles for each day of the month. Having a job of my own to do made me feel grown up and trustworthy. Whenever Dad wanted me to do something, he would always say, "I know you can do this; you're a big man and a big man can do just about anything he wants." Now was my chance to prove to him that I was the big man he always called me.

On Dad's return from the new farm the previous winter, he had told us that the forest abounded with wild game. There were rabbits and grouse and it was going to be my job to catch rabbits to eat. I guess I had done such a good job of it at Cedar Rapids that I had inherited the job, and I was looking forward to it.

Dad had arranged with the new tenant to drive us with the team to the head of the lake on the Old Winter Road. From there Dad would have to build a raft and cross the lake at the narrowest part in order to get to our farm. This was going to be a long and drawn-out move. Dad had walked that old road that had been used years ago by a mining company and had found it encumbered with windfalls and new growth. It would be a lot of work to make it passable.

One day Dad and I were talking and he said, "My friend, I am going to make a settler out of you." He told me that we three men would have to look out for the rest of the family and make sure we all did our share of the work. I interrupted him to ask a question that had been on my mind for some time.

"Is our farm on an island, that we have to get to it by raft?"

Dad took a few minutes to explain: "If we were going to go through town, cross the old red bridge, then continue on down that road that goes for about another mile, we could get to our farm that way. But in doing so, we'd have six miles of deep forest to go through and we'd have to slash a trail. It would take a long time to get there and be a lot of work, so instead we are going by way of the lake."

Then I began to worry about Bully. I felt certain that one mile was a long way to swim–too far for Bully to manage. But Dad assured me he could do it, reminding me of the time Bully fought with the big bull and wound up in the river. Dad had to go with the rowboat to separate them. I remembered that; Bully had nearly drowned that time. But Dad insisted that was because he had been wearing a blindfold and couldn't see where he was going. He promised me we wouldn't let Bully drown swimming across the lake.

After almost a week of preparation, we were ready to leave. We all knew Dad had been very happy lately by the way he sang while he worked, so it was not too surprising when he came to wake us up singing one of the funny little songs he'd make up when he was in a good mood:

"It's daylight in the swamp.
It's time to get up and put your pants on!
There's work to be done,
And I won't do it alone."

I opened my eyes, but it was pitch dark; I thought it was still the middle of the night. I couldn't even see Dad standing in the doorway.

As he turned toward the stairs he told us that Mom had breakfast on the table already and to hurry down before it got cold.

I brushed the sleep from my eyes and groped around in the dark for my socks. I wasn't completely dressed when Paul loped down the stairs, taking two at a time. It seemed that he was just as anxious as I was to leave for the new farm.

When I got down to the kitchen, Paul was gulping down his breakfast and trying to cheer up Mom, who didn't seem to be in a very good mood. Dad was already in the yard waiting for Henry, the new tenant, to arrive. Dad's enthusiasm seemed to perturb Mom even more. She lamented that Dad couldn't wait to get going, just like Paul and me.

Unperturbed, Paul ran out of the door, yelling for me to hurry up, that he and Dad wouldn't wait for me.

Mom grumbled to herself all the time I was eating, saying she didn't know why Dad was taking me with him since I would be more help to her if I stayed. She said, "I just don't know why he wants to leave, especially now that the depression is nearly over. Seems to me we'd be a lot better off here. He could find himself a steady job, and with you boys getting older every year the three of us could look after this farm. In no time we'd have enough money to buy a farm that's already producing, instead of moving into the wilderness." Apparently the "pioneer spirit" hadn't completely taken hold.

I didn't like to hear Mom talk that way. Moving to an undeveloped area sounded like a real adventure to me, and she was trying to take all the fun out of it. I finished my breakfast in a hurry and headed out the door just as the new tenant appeared in the long driveway. Dad was nearly finished with the barn chores and Henry went in to help him. Meanwhile, Paul and I harnessed the team to the wagon. Soon Dad and Henry came out and in no time the load was on and we were ready to leave.

When Dad yelled, "All aboard!" I jumped on the back of the wagon, my legs dangling over the side. Mom shouted to us from the doorway, warning Paul and me to be careful, reminding us that we were no longer just playing a game. I assured her we'd be fine and she would see me again that evening. Finally we began to move, and Dad and Paul picked up their steps with the movement of the wagon. Dad packed the rifle in his hands and Paul carried an axe and a Swede saw across his shoulders. Humming a tune to myself, I watched the farm disappear in the dim morning light.

We soon got on the Old Winter Road, but to me it didn't look like a road at all. Right from the beginning Dad and Paul had to drag windfalls off to the side for us to get by, and every now and then cut a small sapling, too. The team would start, go a short distance and then stop, which made for slow traveling. When the sun reached the treetops, I moved to the middle of the wagon and watched the scenery go by, expecting to see a rabbit or a grouse.

After a while the ride became smoother and it was much easier to follow the road. Dad and Paul had resumed walking behind the wagon and were joking and laughing when one of the horses reared up and began to neigh in terror. I looked up quickly when Henry hollered a warning that there were bears ahead. Then I saw the mother bear and her two cubs. Dad ran to the front of the wagon and fired a shot into the air, which scared the horses as much as it did the bears. But Dad's quick thinking paid off. His shot sent the bears scrambling deeper into the forest for protection. Henry patted the one horse that had been the most skittish, and after a while we got underway again.

About noon we came to a shallow stream and Dad decided we would stop there. Henry fed the team while Dad built a fire to boil water for tea. When it was ready we sat on the edge of the stream and ate our lunch. After resting the team for nearly an hour, we were on our way. The road had improved and we made much better progress. Soon we could see the outline of the lake. I got off the wagon and joined Dad and Paul who were still walking behind. I was so anxious to see the lake that as soon as Dad said, "That's the lake ahead of us," I broke into a run and was almost two hundred feet ahead when I heard Dad call, "Be careful! There could be bears around here. You'd better come back and stay with us."

We didn't see any more wild animals except for a grouse here and there. Finally, we came to the lake. It was the first time I'd ever seen a real lake and I thought it looked much like what I had seen once on a calendar, except this one was more beautiful.

I ran to the beach and stood for a moment, looking at the calm green water glistening in the afternoon sun. After a while I began to run on the golden sand along the shore. I came to a log and sat on it, staring at the far shore, knowing it was our farm that I was looking at. I thought how lucky we were that Dad had found such a beautiful place for us to live. How lucky we were to have a father as talented as he was, to be able to do all the things he could do. He had to be more intelligent than most men because during the depression he never had to ride the freights to look for a job like so many men did. And there was always lots of food on the table, even some left over to feed the hoboes that came knocking at our door begging for a meal.

Almost every day three or four poor, hungry men would knock on the door and ask for something to eat. It got so Mom expected it. They could see the big barn on the outskirts of town and thought we were well-to-do farmers, but they were so wrong. Nevertheless, Mom always had something ready so they never had to wait very long to fill their bellies. She took satisfaction in watching them through the window devouring every bit of food she put on their plates. She knew that some men were too embarrassed to beg for food, so sometimes she would give the others an extra loaf of bread to share with their friends. Seeing these men made me realize how lucky we were. Often we didn't have money to buy clothes, but that didn't seem important as long as we had food on the table.

I was jolted out of my daydreaming when I heard Henry coming with the team and wagon. Dad guided him to a certain spot on the beach and they began to unload. After resting the team for a while, I began the long trek back with Henry. This time I sat up front with him, holding Dad's rifle and keeping an eye out for bears, although I fell asleep once when Henry stopped to rest the horses. It was a long trip back home and it was almost dark when we got back to the farm.

Mom was in the barn milking the cows, so Henry went to help her while I unhitched the team and led the horses to the stable. I took their harness off and filled the manger with hay and their trough with water. Tired as I was, I did all that in record time. I was in a hurry to get to the house and tell the rest of the family about our trip, especially about the encounter with the bears and how beautiful the lake was. Mom didn't let me stay up very late that evening, explaining that it had been a long day for me and it was going to be a long and tiring one again tomorrow.

Being alone in my room that night felt strange. Usually Paul and I would lie in our small cots and talk until sleep came. I got into bed and pulled the blankets over my head to make the room darker, but it didn't help. I could imagine Dad and Paul sleeping on that nice beach by the big bonfire and I wished I were there too. There was so much to think about that sleep didn't come for a long time. For one thing, I was worried about rafting across the lake with Bully; it seemed such a long distance.

Mom didn't have to wake me the next morning. Anxiety had set an alarm in my head and I was awake long before daylight, so I got dressed and tiptoed downstairs. Though I tried to light the stove as quietly as possible, Mom heard me and got up. She remarked that it was not like me to be up so early, that I must be in a hurry to leave. I reminded her that Dad got up at five every morning and I wanted to have the team and Bully fed before Henry arrived. Mom agreed and told me if I would get the cows into the barn she would have my breakfast ready when I got back and then the two of us could do the milking. It was a bit early, but she assured me the cows wouldn't mind.

Henry showed up just as we finished the chores and he was pleased that we could get an early start. He helped carry the buckets to the house and while I went upstairs to pack my clothes he put the milk through the separator. He liked to do that. We both went out to harness the team and pile a huge load of hay onto the wagon. Then we gathered the few remaining items Dad had forgotten. I waved good-bye to Mom and we were on our way.

I think Henry was afraid of bears because as soon as we got on Old Winter Road he asked me to come and sit up front with him and bring the rifle with me.

Although the trip was slow, we made better time than we had on the previous day. As the sun was rising we got to the stream where we'd had lunch the day before. Henry watered the team and rested them for a while before going on. Soon we could see the outline of the lake. I was tempted to run ahead of the team once more but, not wanting to act childish, I remained in my seat. When we got to the beach we all pitched in to unload. I could see some logs scattered about and I knew they were logs Dad and Paul had dragged out of the bush in order to build a raft.

I tied Bully to a tree and gave him a bundle of hay. Then I went to the beach where Dad, Henry and Paul were sitting by a fire waiting for the tea to steep before opening the lunch basket. Henry decided to feed the team, even if it was a bit early, so he wouldn't have to stop along the road on his way back. After eating lunch he wished us luck, got in the wagon and headed back to the farm.

There wasn't much for me to do that afternoon except watch Dad and Paul as they worked on the raft. Dad never liked anyone standing watching him when he worked, so I watched from a distance. He worked quickly because he wanted to finish before it got dark. He and Paul had to reinforce the raft here and there so it would be safe to take the load. It was getting dark when they stopped just long enough to have a bit to eat, then went back to work for perhaps an hour before the raft was ready to go. Dad sat by the fire, lit his pipe and poured himself a cup of black tea. After a while he went back to inspect the raft once more. I guess he was happy with his work because he came back smiling, put the fire out and we got ready for bed.

CHAPTER II

Before going to bed that night we sat on the beach by the fire. I couldn't take my eyes off the lake; it made me feel calm and peaceful just watching the moonlight ripple across the water. Silently I prayed that we would cross it safely. Dad and Paul were talking, but I wasn't interesting in following the conversation. A word caught here and there told me Dad was talking about some of his trapping expeditions. Finally, he dumped the rest of the tea on the fire, making sure every spark was out, and we went to bed. That was my first night's sleep on a bed of boughs, but it wouldn't be my last.

After a sound sleep, I was the first to wake up. I lay on the bed listening to strange noises that I soon realized were the waves lapping on the shore. A light wind had come up during the night and the water was agitated. What if it was too windy to cross? We could be stranded for days.

Dad woke up a bit late and I followed him to the beach where he got the fire going while I went for a bucket of water. Paul got up and led Bully to the lake for a drink, then gave him a bundle of hay. Afterwards he joined us at the fire where Dad was mixing a batch of crepes.

After breakfast we sat around the fire and waited for daylight. As soon as it was light enough Dad began to examine the cedar logs strewn on the beach. Selecting two, he split them and began to whittle. It wasn't long before we had a set of oars and were ready for the crossing.

With long levers, the three of us began to pry the raft toward the water. Dad enjoyed every minute of it, yelling, "Heave Ho!" with every push until, with a last "Heave," the raft was floating.

While Paul and I loaded the raft, Dad tied one log on each side of Bully, joking that he had just invented a cattle life preserver. It looked crude, but it would help Bully stay afloat.

Now came the part I had worried about so much–the first pull on the oars with Bully tied behind the raft. But he didn't hesitate. As soon as the rope tightened around his neck he followed us into the water. Soon he was swimming without any fuss. Dad was happy, saying, "That's what I call smooth sailing," and he began to sing one of his funny little songs:

"There was a sailor man,
Who sailed the deep blue sea.

He sailed from port to port,
His true love to see."

I was beginning to enjoy my first ride on the water when I saw one of Bully's float logs break away. He tilted to one side, but regained his balance. Then the other log broke away, too. Paul and I both yelled at Dad, but he had already seen it. He yelled at me to take the oar so he could help Bully. I grabbed the oar and checked for a landmark, but we were still a long way from shore. Bully was getting panicky; he was trying to swim ahead of the raft and Dad had a hard time controlling him. He hung onto Bully's halter rope and yelled at us to row harder. We did, but the clumsy raft didn't seem to move any faster. Every now and then I turned to check the distance to shore, but it didn't seem to be getting any closer.

Dad was holding Bully's head on the edge of the raft now and I could tell by the tremor in his voice when he'd holler at us to row harder, that he was getting panicky, too. And Paul and I were becoming exhausted. I couldn't feel the tips of my fingers any more but Dad still yelled at us to row harder, while he hung onto Bully's head. The poor bull's eyes were bulging out of their sockets with fear. But just as Dad cried, "We're going to lose him!" Bully's feet touched bottom and he began to stumble ashore. He took few steps and dropped onto the sand with his hind feet still in the water. He lay on his side, panting, eyes still bulging.

We pulled the raft ashore and sat down on the beach to rest. Dad wiped the sweat off his brow and declared, "We nearly lost him." He realized he should have nailed the rope to the logs, but had been in too much of a hurry to think about it. I got up and patted Bully on the flank to let him know we were still with him, but he didn't move; he just stared blankly. Dad told Paul that if he was up to it, they would pack some of the supplies somewhere to establish a camp while I kept an eye on Bully.

Dad and Paul walked up the embankment with heavy packs on their backs and soon disappeared into the forest. I knew it was safe to leave Bully alone for a few minutes, so I walked up the beach as far as the point where the lake widened. Around the point was a beautiful beach with golden sand that gleamed in the sun. I just stood there, savouring the fragrance of the wild roses intermingled with the aroma of cedar and balsam. There were huge white poplars and evergreen trees everywhere. It was the most magnificent sight my eyes had ever seen.

When I returned to the raft Bully was still lying in the same position, but this time he looked at me and he wasn't panting so heavily. Dad and

Paul came back and Dad asked jokingly if I thought they had deserted me. I said I had been so busy exploring I didn't even have time to think about being alone. I mentioned the beach and he said they had seen it, too. He was sure we were going to enjoy life on our new farm. Then the two of them disappeared into the forest once more.

After they were gone I climbed the embankment and walked along the freshly-cut trail to get a better look at our farm. All I saw were trees and more trees. To my amazement I found myself in the middle of a virgin forest with tall poplar bordering the lake, and spruce, balsam and cedar further inland. How would it ever become a farm? And what would Mom say when she saw the forest? I was afraid she might not even want to stay in such isolation, where there wasn't a human being for miles. In fact, if one of us was injured and we had to get help, we would have to trek seven miles through deep forest. As young as I was, I didn't think this was a place to bring a woman.

Then I began thinking about wildlife and I remembered the encounter with bears on Old Winter Road. I was sure there would be bears around here, too, so I quickly turned back to the safety of the lake. Running wildly, I roused a flock of grouse right in front of me and nearly fainted.

Back at the beach I saw Bully walking slowly toward the point, stopping now and then to look at the lake, and I wondered what *his* thoughts were. Leading him back to the raft I tied him to some willows and then sat down to wait for Dad and Paul. They weren't long in coming and Dad was excited. "We've found a real nice camping spot near a small stream," he said. "You won't have far to go for fresh water." Then he added, "I see Bully decided to get up. Good. Now we can all grab a pack and head out. We still have a big job ahead of us to build a camp for the night."

Dad tied a few bundles of hay together and slung them across Bully's back. He handed me a light pack and I followed him and Paul, who was leading Bully, down the narrow trail. After about fifteen minutes we came to the place Dad had chosen and he was right, it was a really nice spot. Situated among tall poplar trees, it was near the small stream he had mentioned and about fifty feet from the lake.

"This is it, my friends," Dad said. "This is where we are going to stay while we build the log house. The two of you can pack in what's left on the raft. I'm going to build us a shelter to sleep in."

When Paul and I came back from the raft with a load, Dad had felled a few poplars, cut them into twelve-foot lengths, and was splitting them in half. He propped them against a rafter he had fastened to a couple of poplars about ten feet apart, and it wasn't long before he had a lean-to built. He told me to pack some stones from the shore to build a fire pit while he and Paul went to the lake and rowed the raft around the point to the campsite. Then I was to cut some boughs for our bed while Paul was building a stall for Bully so we could keep him tied safely. When everything was ready, Dad cooked our supper and we sat on a log to eat our first meal on our new farm.

After smoking his pipe, Dad sent Paul to cut firewood for the night while he and I went to set the fishing net. He showed me step by step how to do it. First he cut down and stripped two trees about twelve feet long and made two notches on each: one about three feet from the bottom for the sinker line and another four feet higher up where the other end of the net was fastened. Using a wooden hammer, he drove the first pole about a foot and a half into the soft mud at the bottom of the lake. "Now" he said, "gently pole the raft while you unfold the net into the water."

When the net was completely unrolled, the ends were attached to the other pole at the notches. Then, with the net stretched as tightly as possible so it would hang evenly in the water, we drove the pole deep into the mud where it would catch bottom fish as well. Dad clapped me on the back. "Well done," he said. "From now on, it's your job."

We went to bed in the lean-to, but it wasn't long before we moved to the hard ground by the fire where the smoke kept away the ferocious mosquitoes. Dad was up early, as usual, so he lit the fire and cooked breakfast As soon as he had eaten he began building a stone boat to haul the hay.

Stone boats were made out of hardwood logs–in our case, birch–eight to ten feet long. The logs were hewn at both ends so the boat could be dragged from either end by one horse or a team. It had three beams across, one at the very front, one in the middle and one at the very back. The beams were hewn to form an arch at the bottom for clearance, and fastened to runners shaped like those of a sleigh, using hardwood dowels.

Paul came with me to retrieve the net, which was loaded with fish of all kinds. I had never seen so many fish–a lot more than we could use. By the time we hung the net to dry Dad had finished the stone boat. He and Paul got on the raft and headed across the lake to get some more hay Dad asked me to harness Bully and drag the stone boat to the landing where he and Paul could load it with hay when they got back.

That done I sat around for awhile, but soon got restless. I decided to gather some deadwood and dam the creek with wood and mud. Soon the water began to rise until it formed a good-sized basin. I was still admiring my dam when Dad and Paul returned. Dad exclaimed, "What do you know, a family of beavers has moved in!" Then he added, "You did a real good job. Now when you catch more fish than we can use, you can release them in there and we'll always have fresh fish to eat."

Paul and I crossed the lake twice that day to get the rest of the hay while Dad began to clear an area to build the log house. Time went quickly and before we knew it, it was getting dark. Dad cooked a delicious supper of fish and pan-fried potatoes and I ate so much I could barely move.

The next day Paul and Dad worked on the house while I was left at camp again to wash the dishes and do the cleaning up. That done, I harnessed Bully and began hauling hay. There was such a big stack of it that it took me all day and I was glad when I finished. I lighted the fire and rested for awhile, but soon got tired of waiting for Dad and Paul. I fed Bully early and took a walk to see how the house was coming along. They were working hard, rolling big logs up to the house to add one more round to the walls. I stayed out of their way so Dad wouldn't yell at me, and I was glad when he asked me to get Bully and skid a couple logs that were too far for them to reach. I always felt good when Dad asked me to do something new, and was proud when I did it to his satisfaction. Also, it made me take more interest in what was going on.

We returned to camp tired and hungry after a long day's work. As he was cooking supper Dad told me I had done well and I could see he was happy with my work. He said as soon as he had some spare time he was going to build me a smaller raft to set the net. He knew the big one was much too hard for me to handle and, at any rate, they would have to use it when it came time to move the family.

We were so busy there was never much time to loaf around or get lonesome. But one day when I had all my chores done early I decided to sit on my favourite rock and relax by the lake. I lay on my back on the big rock, watching the clouds roll by, but my mind was never idle for a second. I began to think about how we were going to get to school, but as hard as I tried, I just couldn't come up with a solution. It looked impossible. Perhaps our school days were over and I would never have a chance to learn divisions. Sitting on that rock, thinking about school, I realized how much I had been looking forward to going back in the fall.

It was almost dark when Dad and Paul came back. Dad was in a good mood, as he had been lately, always laughing and joking. He was teasing Paul, who had fallen in a mud hole and was caked with the stuff from head to foot, including his face. They were still laughing when I went to bed and I had to pull the covers over my head to muffle the sound so I could sleep.

The next morning Dad told me how to build a shelter to keep the rain off Bully. He pointed out four spruce trees that were fairly well spaced and left me to it. I tied a pole, or stringer, to two trees, then another pole a little lower to the two trees opposite, much as he had done for the lean-to. With a good slant to the roof, I placed some poles across the stringers and covered them with moss. The shelter was completed in a few days and I didn't think I had done such a great job, but it met with Dad's approval.

We had been at the new farm for a little more than two weeks and much had been accomplished. The walls of the house were up and land cleared around it. Unfortunately, there was also a lot of mud because of a heavy rain the day before.

Early in the afternoon I took a walk through the forest, and a couple of hundred feet from the house I came upon a huge water hole where there were three big jets bubbling on the surface. I rushed back to tell Dad and was disappointed when he told me he had already seen it.

"That's a natural spring," he said. "That's where we are going to get our drinking water. You can take an axe and cut a trail to it if you think you're man enough." That was just the challenge I needed to get started. I took the axe and went to work immediately. After that I did many small jobs that I felt were helpful. For example, one day Dad asked me to harness Bully and gather some moss to chink the house. Paul was doing the chinking and I easily kept up with him bringing load after load of moss.

We had been at the site for more than a month and the house was nearly finished. Dad still had to put the roof on and the floor in, as well as the windows and doors, but he would do that when he came back from town with the necessary lumber and hardware. He was pleased that we had built a log house thirty-eight by twenty-four feet in just over a month. But it was the middle of September, the nights were getting colder, and still there was a lot of work to be done before we could move in. We would have to hurry to stay ahead of the frost.

Dad was always especially nice when he wanted me to do something I might be afraid to tackle, or have good reason to say no to. He'd always begin by praising me like he did one evening when the three of us were sitting by the fire. For a long time he was quiet and pensive, then he began his smooth approach. Looking straight at me, he said, "My friend, I have a very important job for you to do. It's a job only a big man like you wouldn't be afraid of doing, that's why I'm asking you to do it. It would sure help us all out a lot."

I didn't wait for Dad to ask me what it was he wanted me to do, nor to finish complimenting me. I was ready to tackle anything he asked. "Sure, Dad," I said eagerly. "I can do anything you ask me to do. I'm not a little boy any more."

"Well," he said, "we've gone as far as we can go with the house for now. We need lumber, windowpanes and some hardware and I have to go to town to get them. If I take Paul with me, he could start packing while I get the supplies and we'd move the family at the same time. It would save me another trip to town. You know winter isn't very far away and we can't waste any time. But someone has to stay here to look after Bully and the camp. All you would have to do is feed Bully. There's lots of food for you to eat; I made three big bannocks last night that should last until we get back. We won't be gone for more than four or five days and then we'll be back with the family." We agreed that I would stay.

The next day Dad and Paul finished as much as they could on the house. Before going to bed that evening Dad asked me, "Are you afraid to stay here alone?"

I said, "No, I'm not afraid. We've been here nearly six weeks and I haven't seen anything bigger than a rabbit."

Dad assured me there was nothing to be afraid of and I wasn't in any danger as long as I didn't wander into the bush or go out on the raft.

The next morning, long before daylight, Dad was up cooking breakfast for himself and Paul. It was still dark when they left but I got up to say goodbye. Dad promised again that they would be back in four or five days at the most. That wasn't a very long time to be alone, I thought, as I watched them disappear down the trail with Paul carrying their lunch in a small packsack.

That first day went by quickly and it was the next morning before it really struck home that I was alone. I sat on my favourite rock by the lake, feeling very empty inside. It was going to be a long week for me.

After a while I went back to the lean-to and made a notch on a tree–day one. Little did I know there would be six notches on that tree before I saw my family.

Night came, even if I didn't want it to. This was the part of the day I dreaded most; it was so much lonelier during these evening hours–hours that seemed endless as I sat and waited for that sleepy feeling to come over me. My motions became automatic: first, pork and beans for supper, then stoke the fire and add a few extra logs so it would burn longer. I stretched out on the bed, facing the flames, and watched the sparks fly in all directions until I went to sleep.

Awake long before daylight, I stayed in bed until hunger made me get up. I fed and watered Bully and made myself breakfast, but there wasn't much else to do. I remembered Dad telling me that Paul had left a Swede saw hanging in a tree and I should place it under shelter somewhere so it wouldn't rust. Riding Bully to the log house, I walked around the back and spotted the saw. As I was walking back with the saw I noticed what I thought were dog tracks in the mud, lots of tracks. Puzzled by my discovery, I reasoned it must be stray dogs that had gotten lost chasing wild game. For a long time, I called, "Rover! Here Rover!" and "Here Teddy!" but there was no response. Probably they had found their way home by now, I reasoned.

After taking care of the saw I rode Bully back to camp, then went to the dam to see how many fish were left. Dad had warned me not to go on the raft he had built for me, but I was just looking for an excuse to set the net. However, there were lots of fish left.

Gaffing a big pickerel, I dressed it to eat the next day with pan-fried potatoes and bannock. Bannock was a popular staple in the woods and we always had a mix on hand. It was made with flour, baking powder and salt, with enough water added to make a thick dough. And it was easy to cook: you place a frying pan over the fire, add plenty of fat, spread the batter over the pan and cook until it browns and rises, then flip over and brown on the other side.

While planning my meal, I kept thinking about home. The rest of my family were together, talking happily about the big move, and here I was all alone, wishing I were with them. How long will it be, I wondered, before they get back? Will they make it before the weather changes? September, usually a wet, windy, cold month, had been nice so far except for a few days of rain.

That night, making sure I had lots of firewood by the pit, I dropped a couple of green logs on the fire so it would burn slowly, and went to bed feeling very sad and lonely. Dad always said, "If you're good and tired, you'll sleep like a baby," but as tired as I was, sleep wouldn't come. Not that I was scared, or even nervous, just that my mind kept wandering. If it wasn't about missing school, it was about how long before they all came back. Some ghost stories even came to mind and I couldn't get rid of them. I wasn't afraid of ghosts–didn't even believe in them–but at the same time, thinking about them didn't exactly lull me to sleep. Perhaps it was the stillness of the night that kept me awake. Everything was so quiet, not a wisp of a breeze; even the loon that was always in the bay was silent that night. Eventually I dozed off, but not for long.

I was awakened by the most horrifying sounds I had ever heard. Startled, I sat up in bed. My hair felt like it was standing on end. There was an eerie quiet for a few minutes and I thought I must have been dreaming, but it came again and again, sounding as if it were right behind the lean-to. The second time I heard the baying I didn't need anyone to tell me I was surrounded by a pack of wolves. Dad had described their howls to us while recounting some of his trapping stories.

Hampered by the dark, I groped under the pallet for the rifle I knew Dad always kept fully loaded. It wasn't anywhere under the boughs where it usually was. Frantically, I searched every corner of the bed on my hands and knees, but it wasn't there. Obviously, Dad had hidden it somewhere before leaving, afraid I might play with it and hurt myself. The fire was nearly out and I was too scared to go outside and put more wood on it. Pulling the blankets over my head to muffle the howls, I lay down again, every part of my body shaking.

After a few minutes I summoned up enough courage to get to my knees and peek outside. My blood froze. At a distance of less than two hundred feet, three wolves were sitting side by side, another standing a few feet away and, much farther, still another who appeared to be doing most of the howling.

Looking toward the fire pit I saw the axe leaning against a log. I ran as fast as I could, grabbed the axe and ran back to the lean-to, crouching in the corner. Eons passed before the howling began to fade and when I peeked again three of the wolves got to their feet, obeying the call of the other wolf who appeared to be the leader. As I watched through the cracks of the lean-to I saw in the dim moonlight the four wolves join their leader and slowly move away. But it was a long time before I could relax.

When I thought they were at a safe distance I ran to the fire pit and loaded it with wood. Dad used to tell us that wolves were afraid of fire and if we were ever cornered by a pack, to light a fire and stand near it. Soon the flames were billowing out of the pit and rising high into the air.

I spent the rest of the night sitting on a log by the fire, wondering about things. Mainly I wondered why my dad, having spent so many years in the bush, didn't know there might be wolves in the area. And if he did know, why he didn't warn me about them. Had I known, I would have been better prepared and I wouldn't have been so scared. Finally, exhausted, I fell asleep still sitting on the log.

Bully's mooing woke me up. He was hungry. When I tried to get up I realized my neck was sore and my legs were stiff from the position in which I had been sleeping. Looking at the sky I could see it was well past noon and I was hungry, too, but I had to feed Bully first.

I didn't go anywhere that day, but prepared to defend myself against any further onslaught by wolves. Intending to keep the fire burning all night, I gathered lots of firewood. Logs that were left over from building the lean-to were used to block the entrance. A butcher knife was tied to a long pole to use as a spear. After sawing logs and packing heavy bolts to make the place safe, literally working like a beaver, I was dead tired.

After supper I went to bed, but was afraid to go to sleep. I decided to lead Bully to the lake for a drink, then tie him near the fire where he might be safer. But when we got to the lake, the perfect solution to our problem came to me. What if I made my bed on the raft for the night? I could leave Bully on the beach, tied to a long rope. The other end of the rope would be tied to the raft lying in shallow water a few feet from the beach. The raft would be well secured if it were anchored by posts hammered into the bottom of the lake. And, if the wolves came back, all I had to do was pull on the rope and lead Bully into the lake where he would be safe.

Just thinking of such a perfect plan made me very proud. I packed a bunch of hay on the raft for my bed and, in case it got cold during the night, took some firewood and the bottom part of a barrel we used to burn smudges to keep the mosquitoes away. Feeling reassured about my safety and Bully's, I sat by the fire until late in the evening, then led Bully to the beach. Pushing the raft about twenty feet from shore, I anchored it well so it wouldn't drift away during the night. After the fire was lighted in the barrel, I lay on my back, hands crossed over my chest, staring at the sky and marveling at my ingenuity.

While waiting for sleep to come I made plans for the next day. I would hitch Bully to the stone boat and go to the landing so I could see the wagon arrive with everyone on board.

No sooner had I gone to sleep than the loon, who was back in the bay, woke me up with its mournful call. I hated loons and wished this one would go away. Its call sounded like someone in distress. In fact, it reminded me of one spring night on the priest's farm when the river had overflown its banks. We were at the dinner table when we heard someone calling for help. We all ran outside to listen. The call came from across the river so Dad got in the leaky old punt and rowed in the direction from which the call came. He found a man in the water, a non-swimmer whose boat had sunk. The man had been hanging onto some willows for a long time and was about to let go. He would have drowned had Dad not rescued him. I could only hope that the sound I heard really was a loon, as I was in no position to rescue anyone.

The sun was high overhead when I awoke. I was still tired and my ribs were sore from the logs of the raft. The hay had slipped into the water through the spaces between the logs and I had been lying on bare wood. Looking toward the beach I could see Bully still lying on his side, chewing his cud. I poled the raft to shore, put Bully back in his stall and placed a bundle of hay in front of him.

After cooking breakfast and washing the dishes, I felt too restless to wait until afternoon so I harnessed Bully to the stone boat and left for the landing. Sitting on my favourite high rock I stared at the opposite shore until my eyes were burning, but nothing new had been added to the pile of hay that was there before.

Just before the sun reached the treetops in the west, I hooked Bully to the stone boat again and returned to the lean-to in order to get ready for another night's sleep on the raft. But we wouldn't spend that night on the water. In the middle of eating my meal, a strong wind came up and it kept getting stronger with every gust. I gulped the last of my dinner and ran to the beach to pull the raft as far as I could onto the sand so it wouldn't be destroyed by the waves. Then I got Bully out of his stall and tied him near the fire pit so he would be closer to me if the wolves came back.

We couldn't have a fire because the wind might carry the sparks and start a forest fire–something Dad had warned me about. I felt trapped: nowhere to go and nothing I could do to change the situation. I sat outside by Bully for a long time, hanging onto my homemade spear. After a while I began to doze, so I gave up and went to bed.

The wind was still blowing in the morning, but more moderately. The fire was out, of course, so I hurried to light it. I was starving and wanted my breakfast. While I was eating, I reflected on how silly I had been to worry about wolves, the wind, and starting a forest fire. It was so silly that I wouldn't even mention it to anyone; besides, this was the last day I would be here alone. Dad had said four days and today was the fourth. After making another notch on the poplar, I told myself: *When the sun gets overhead, I am going to the landing again. I am sure I'll see them coming up the old road long before the sun gets to the treetops.*

Before washing the dishes I led Bully to the lake for a drink. We were almost to the lake when I noticed a family of Indians that had camped on the beach for the night. I walked back, tied bully in his stall, and returned to the lean-to. I was a bit afraid of Indians. I remembered my mother telling us that some Indians would steal kids and they were never seen again. At any rate, I wasn't about to mess with them; I'd had enough trouble this week as it was.

I was stooped by the fire, poking around in the ashes, when I looked up and saw a small but stocky Indian standing nearby. He wore a pair of heavy navy blue wool pants, moccasins, a suit coat that was much too small for him, and a towel wrapped around his neck. He smiled and said something I didn't understand so I just shrugged my shoulders. He took a pipe out of his pocket and pointed to the bowl with his finger, saying something that sounded like "bacco bogan." After he repeated the phrase several times, I got the idea: he wanted some tobacco for his pipe.

Not wanting to argue the matter, I went to the stump where Dad kept his tobacco buried in the moss to keep it fresh. The Indian's face beamed when I gave him a handful of leaf tobacco. He turned to go back and motioned for me to follow him. He was quite insistent so, reluctant as I was, I felt I had no choice but to do so. When we got to the lake I saw his wife and a boy about my age, but neither of them paid any attention to me. The man raised a tarp that was covering a hindquarter of moose meat and motioned to me to take it. Then he just stood there and laughed as I tried with all my might to lift the meat, but it was much too heavy for me. When he saw that I really couldn't budge the meat he stopped laughing, picked it up and carried it to the lean-to. After dropping it on the ground, he quickly turned around and pranced back toward the lake, laughing once again.

Now that I could see the meat more closely, I realized it had been dried by the fire and would keep for a long time.

When I looked again toward the beach, I saw the three of them paddle away along the shore. That was my first encounter with these friendly, generous people. I wished that Dad had been there as he may have been able to talk with them. I knew by some of the stories he told that he could converse with Indians of the Ojibwa tribe, which was the tribe that was in our area.

Hungry by now, I dismantled my spear so I could use the knife to cut myself a moose steak. The meat looked red and juicy inside so I lost no time in trimming the rind off and tossing the steak in the frying pan. This was my first taste of red meat in a very long time and it was delicious. Again I tried to lift the hindquarter, but wasn't able to. It would have to stay where it was until Dad got back.

On a full stomach things didn't look so bad. Maybe my luck was changing.

Early the next day I packed a big lunch, harnessed Bully and went to the landing once again. Sitting on the big rock, I could see if any action took place on the opposite shore. Nothing. I fed Bully and had lunch myself and waited some more. The sun was going down and I was on my way to harness Bully when I saw the team appear on the crest of the hill and make its way toward the beach. Heart pounding, I turned around, wiped my eyes to make sure I could see properly, and looked again. Yes! It was the team! I climbed back on the rock, jumped up and down, waved my arms and yelled. Finally someone on the wagon saw me and began to shout back. It was Henry and Paul with a load of furniture. I stayed long enough to watch them unload and head back.

Deeply disappointed, I returned to the lean-to. It was too late in the day for them to make another trip. The best thing for me to do was to clean up and make sure everything was ready when they arrived tomorrow. I made a good job of it, even sweeping the ground with a broom Dad had made out of cedar boughs. I covered the meat with a piece of canvas and then checked the dam to see how many fish were left. There were only three, so I set the net to replenish our supply.

There was a gentle breeze blowing from the south and I may have been able to sleep on the raft that night but I was afraid a wind might come up. I tied Bully near the fire pit and sat beside him, talking to him as if he were a human being.

Dawn arrived, cold and windy, but Bully and I were prepared to spend another day on the landing. Late in the afternoon, just as I was beginning to lose hope, the team appeared over the crest of the hill. My eyes focused fiercely on the wagon, willing there to be more than two people on it, but it was Henry and Paul again. They began to unload on the beach but I didn't wave or try to attract their attention. They wouldn't have heard me anyhow, above the wind.

Returning to the lean-to, I built a fire and sat by it for a long time. I wasn't hungry, just sad and dejected, almost to the point of tears. It wasn't fair! I had kept my part of the bargain; why couldn't Dad keep his part, too?

Engrossed in self-pity, I didn't notice at first that the wind had died down and it had begun to rain. As usual, I checked on Bully before settling down for the night, but he wasn't in his stall. I hadn't tied him properly and he'd gotten loose and wandered away. Grabbing the axe, I began to follow his tracks that were going toward the log house. But from there, there were so many tracks I couldn't distinguish the old ones from the fresh. Which direction should I go? There wasn't that much daylight left, so I would have to hurry. Finally I heard a faint mooing that seemed to come from the direction of the spring. Heading that way at a full run, I found Bully not very far up the trail. His halter rope was snarled in the root of a stump and he was unable to move. After calling him a few choice names, I got on his back and rode him to his stall where I made sure he was tied fast.

Hungry by then, I grabbed a piece of stale bannock, sprinkled brown sugar on it and gulped it down, standing with my back to the fire so I could dry off.

Lying in bed that night, I began to feel sorry for myself again–sorry for the situation I had gotten myself into. I couldn't blame Dad; he was only trying to make things a bit easier for all of us, but did I have to be so eager to accept responsibility? It was all my own fault; I was always too willing to help.

The next day the rain had stopped and it looked like a nice day ahead. Another notch on the big poplar–day six. I fed Bully and had my own breakfast and it was while I was standing by the fire that morning that my thoughts began flying in all directions. What if they were never coming back? What if they had deserted me, left me there alone with winter just around the corner? I would have to make the lean-to a lot warmer in order to survive the cold winter nights. I'd have to learn on my own how to catch rabbits to eat. The lake would be frozen, so I couldn't set the net. I'd have to catch lots of fish now and freeze them. Suddenly I was very aware of my own survival.

Automatically, I harnessed Bully, put some hay on the stone boat, packed a lunch and slowly headed to the landing. This time there were no expectations. If they arrived today, fine; if they didn't, my attitude was: there's nothing I can do about it.

About half way to the landing a large horse-like animal thundered across our path. Immediately I stopped Bully, although he didn't see to be afraid. The animal disappeared through the forest at a fast lope and, when I had time to think about it, I knew what it was from Dad's descriptions. I was thrilled to have seen my first live moose.

When we got to the landing I didn't bother taking the harness off Bully but just tied him to some willows and left him with a bit of hay. I took my position on the big rock, getting down to run on the beach whenever I got cold. It would have been a lot more comfortable staying by the fire at the lean-to.

Much earlier than I expected, I saw the team rounding the crest of the hill. They must have left the farm long before daylight. Straining my eyes, I tried to see if there were more than two on the wagon this time, and there were. I counted three heads above the huge load and two walking, one on each side of the wagon.

It seemed like an eternity before the wagon reached the beach and when it did I could see Gemma and Noella running like the wind on the beach. Counting everyone as they got off the wagon, I saw Mom carrying Roland, and Donat trying to keep up to Gemma and Noella. Dad, Henry and Paul were unloading the wagon and packing things on the raft.

I wasn't cold anymore. I kept on jumping up and down, waving my arms and yelling. Gemma spotted me and waved back. Finally they all got on the raft and, as they came closer, Dad called to me, "Leave Bully there and go make us something to eat. We're all starving!"

CHAPTER III

The words were barely out of Dad's mouth before I was running up the embankment. In fact, I ran so fast the wind made my eyes fill with water and I stumbled and fell two or three times.

Back at camp I went straight to the vegetable pit Dad had dug for the potatoes and carrots. Picking out eight of the largest potatoes, I buried them in the hot ashes at the base of the fire. I figured I had less than an hour before the family arrived so I hurriedly pared a few carrots and put them on to boil, then cut some steaks, making sure to cut the crusty rind off each slice.

After the potatoes had been baking for almost half and hour I put a few steaks in a frying pan over the open flames, but I was in such a hurry I couldn't do anything right. I dropped the pot of carrots into the fire, spilling some of the water onto the flame and nearly putting out the fire. Then I burned my finger trying to turn a steak over. Licking the burn, I carried on. I was doing the last of the steaks when I heard Dad's voice. I looked up to say, "Hi," and proceeded to drop the whole pan of steaks into the fire. Dad began to laugh. I picked up the steaks, wiped off the ashes and placed the meat back in the pan.

I stood up and saw Gemma and Noela running toward me; they both gave me a big hug. Farther away Mom was walking carefully, carrying Roland in her arms while holding onto Donat's hand. As soon as Dad got close enough to the fire pit to get a smell of the meat cooking, he knew it was moose and asked how I came to have a hindquarter of moose meat. I told him about the family of Indians that had camped on the beach and that I had traded some of his tobacco for it.

Dad unloaded the packsack from his shoulders and took out two loaves of freshly-baked bread and a large container of butter. He laid it all on a log, then told me that the chef was back and I should sit down while he finished the rest of the meal.

Dad dug the potatoes out of the ashes. They were still hard, so he sliced them and finished cooking them in the frying pan over the flames. When they were done he told us to dig in. We filled our plates and found a spot to sit–on a log or on the ground–and began to eat.

Paul arrived with Bully and the stone boat loaded with lumber. He just grabbed a steak and kept on going toward the log house, gnawing on his steak as he went. Dad didn't waste any time; he barely had swallowed his last mouthful when he was on his way to join Paul, telling the rest of us to just relax.

I didn't sit around for very long, either. I went to the log house and began to work on the roof with Paul while Dad worked on the doors and windows. There was so much left to be done on the house and we knew Dad needed all the help he could get.

After a few days Mom began to worry about the frost setting in. She wanted to have enough land cleared to put in a garden in the spring, so I began to work with her, slashing and pulling stumps, stacking them in big piles and burning them. Day after day we worked from dawn to dark until the ground was frozen so hard we couldn't do any more. We had managed to clear almost one acre of land, which was a lot more than she needed for a garden.

Now that we were getting heavy frost Dad wanted me to set the net every day so we could freeze fish for the winter. He also took time to show me how to make and set rabbit snares and to freeze the rabbits as well. There was a lot of work to be done. Dad and Paul were building a barn for Bully, who needed a warm place for the winter.

Dad, who was very good with a broad axe, hewed poplar logs to build a barn with a large loft where we could store the hay. After many days' work it was completed and I thought the barn looked better than the log house!

While Dad and Paul worked on the barn, I was busy cutting firewood for the long winter months ahead. But one morning Dad said, "My friend, you and I are going moose hunting this morning."

Paul stayed behind to take my place cutting firewood. I was excited to be going with Dad. He led the way with his rifle and his packsack and I followed, carrying an axe and a smaller packsack.

About two miles from the house we came to a small hill covered with a dusting of snow where Dad saw some moose tracks. He told me to stay there and not make a sound while he went ahead. I waited for a long time and was beginning to get really cold when I heard some rifle shots–four altogether. I was sure Dad had missed and we'd have to go home empty-handed. But a few minutes after I'd heard the shots, I saw Dad appear through the trees and he told me he'd been very lucky. "We have four moose to dress and carry all the way home, so we'd better get busy."

Dad started working on a moose while I watched closely in order to learn how it was done. I knew I would have to do it myself one day. Dad placed two of the livers in my packsack and two in his. He rolled one of the skins and tied it with twine, telling me that he needed the skin to make rawhide to lace the snowshoes we would need during the winter.

After getting the meat dressed and hung in trees so the foxes wouldn't be able to get at it, he said, "My friend, we have done a super job this morning so we are going to eat our lunch in style." He built a fire and we ate our lunch. After lighting his pipe, he asked me if I wanted to go for a walk–to do a bit of exploring, as he would always say.

We walked for about a half a mile before coming to a huge muskeg. There were lots of dead trees and other small ones growing on clumps of moss here and there. We didn't go any farther. After having a good look around Dad said, "Let's go back and we'll head for home." No need to say what we all had for supper that night.

There was never a dull moment on the new farm; there was always something to do. Sometimes we didn't like doing what we were told to, but we did it anyway and we all got along well.

One morning Dad said to me, "You are going to cut firewood today while Paul comes with me to help pack the meat home. He can carry a lot more than you." I was disappointed, but accepted Dad's order. Before they left Dad filled a tub with water, added some soap, and put the moose skin in to soak. He would leave it there for six or seven days, or until the hair began to loosen so it could be scraped off. Then we would have rawhide.

Dad and Paul brought the meat home, but the next time Dad went out Paul stayed behind to cut firewood and Dad took me with him. We were looking for suitable wood to make snowshoe frames. Again, I walked behind him, packing the lunch and carrying the axe.

We had walked at least five miles through the forest when we came to a river and there, along the bank, was the wood we wanted. Dad felled two white ash trees, split and trimmed a half dozen strips and tied them together. We walked home dragging the strips behind us.

With the urgent work done, we could relax a little, but we still needed firewood for the winter. Dad and Paul did the sawing and splitting while I packed the wood to the house and piled it near the porch so it would be easily accessible.

One day Dad tested the moose hide, pronounced it ready, and began to scrape the hair from the hide. With the hair removed, he sliced the hide in long, narrow strips until he had a mountain of "babishe," as he called it. He made three sets of snowshoe frames from the ash tree, lacing them with the strips of moose hide. Always very proud of his workmanship, Dad would hang each pair on the wall as they were finished. After admiring his work for awhile, Dad said to Mom, "Aren't you lucky to have a man who can do such nice work?"

Mom replied, "If you're so good at doing things, you can clean up the mess you've made in the house."

There wasn't much privacy in our house. The three bedrooms were all on one side, separated by rough lumber. The largest bedroom was for Mom and Dad, although Donat and Roland slept there, too; one was for Noella and Gemma, nearer the heater because Noella was frail and always felt cold, and Paul and I shared the one in the far corner.

Whenever Mom and Dad had an argument, they always had it in their bedroom and tried to keep their voices low, but once in awhile they would be so agitated we could hear some heated words. We all knew they were having a few arguments lately. We didn't worry much about it because we knew most of their arguments were about money—a shortage of it; money needed to buy clothes, for instance. We didn't have many clothes, which bothered Mom. Gemma and Noella had a few changes of clothing, but Paul and I had one pair of pants each, two shirts, one set of underwear and one pair of shoes. My shoes were fairly good, but Paul's were full of holes. Mom had two dresses, one red-and-white checked, the other blue-and-white checked, both of which she had made out of flour bags.

One evening we heard Dad say loudly as he came out of the bedroom, "I owe nearly one hundred dollars at the grocery store that I promised to pay in the spring and I won't have my credit go bad for one hundred dollars. I'm going to earn the money to pay that bill if it kills me."

A couple of days after that argument Dad said to me, "My friend, you and me are going trapping this winter to see if we can make a few dollars. We are going to leave Paul here to look after the family. He is more able than you to go for help if it is needed and he can keep busy doing some slashing and cutting firewood. I'm sure you'd prefer to be in the bush with me." Actually, I would have preferred to stay home and look after my rabbit snares, but I didn't say so.

Mom and Dad were very different and probably should not have married. Mom had a mediocre education, but she had a good business head and was comfortable with people. She was Bertha Frechette, from a French family, with one uncle who was a famous poet and served in parliament in Ottawa. Two of her uncles were priests and two aunts were nuns. Dad was Napoleon Desbiens, known as "Nap." He was very talented in many ways and could flourish where others perished, but wasn't comfortable around people and preferred a secluded life. All he knew was hard work and how to feed his family. He was one-quarter Iroquois on his mother's side and had not been to school one day in his life. Mom had to sign her name below his 'X.'

Before Dad left for town one morning he asked Mom if she needed anything. If she did, he said, he would put it on the bill, but Mom told him she didn't need a thing.

When Dad came back later that day with his packsack nearly full of groceries, he began to pull out supplies: salted pork, macaroni, brown sugar, five pounds of tea, and a lot of pipe tobacco. Mom wasn't too excited because she knew that most of the supplies were for the trap line and not for the house, but Dad had a surprise for her: at the very bottom of the sack was a pair of galoshes. When Dad handed them to her she jumped with joy and exclaimed, "At last I have a pair of shoes to wear outside!" The bitterness of their arguments was forgotten at that moment.

At dinner that evening Dad said to me, "Day after next we are going to head across the lake, you and me, and find us a nice place to trap for the winter–not too far from here so we can come home for a visit now and then. We are going to make a lot of money trapping mink and martens."

The next night I went to bed early so I'd be well rested for the day ahead. From my bedroom I could hear Mom tell Dad not to be too hard on me, that I was still just a boy. Dad said, "He's ten and at that age I had already been working for three years. At seven I was hauling logs with a team." Mom told him that was no excuse, and he was not to take it out on me.

Dad woke me up when it was still very dark outside. There was a large packsack by the door, a smaller one next to it, and two pairs of snowshoes, although we wouldn't need them yet as there was only a few inches of snow on the ground. As soon as we finished breakfast we were ready to leave, but Mom took a few minutes to admonish Dad not to take me on any of his long exploration treks and to make sure I was dressed warmly whenever we were outside. The lecture over, we strapped on our packsacks. Dad told Mom we weren't going very far and would be back for sure at Christmas, if not before. He said, "We'll find a good spot where there will be enough marten to pay for our grocery bill." The dark brown fur of the weasel-like marten was easily sold for use as a neckpiece or to trim coats.

We crossed the iced-over lake with our heavy packsacks, bedroll and tent. Following the shoreline for a few miles, we came to a good spot to enter the forest where walking was fairly easy. However, it became more difficult as we went along and Dad had to cut a trail to make it easier for me, which slowed us down. The longer we walked, the deeper the snow, until it was almost ankle deep. When we stopped for lunch Dad looked for marten tracks, but there were none. We walked until dark, when we came to a big white spruce with long limbs that almost touched the ground. Dad decided it would make a good shelter for the night.

As we were eating breakfast the next morning Dad assured me we wouldn't have to go much farther. He said, "I'm sure we'll see marten tracks not too far from here." But we didn't. Late in the afternoon we came to a small lake that looked more like a slough of stagnant water in the middle of a muskeg. It was surrounded by small black spruce and the ground was covered with thick moss, into which we sank deeply as we walked. Dad had been looking for water and this was the first we had come to. "Now," he said, "we'll try to find a good spot to put the tent for the winter."

We walked for almost a mile around the lake before finding a higher spot where there was some dry wood, and there we pitched the tent. It was dark by the time we were finished so we had supper by the fire and went to bed. I was fast asleep as soon as I lay down.

When I awoke next morning Dad was leaving the tent. He told me to stay around camp that day, that he wasn't going to be gone long. He was just going to look for the best spot to start setting traps. I waited the whole day, cutting dry firewood just for something to do. By the time he returned at dusk, I was really getting bored.

"My friend," Dad said, "we have come to the right place. Today I killed a moose, so we'll have plenty of meat to eat, and I found a real good spot to set traps. We're going to start first thing in the morning."

Dad and I left early, packing a big lunch. Dad had a dozen traps in his packsack, along with some moose liver for bait, and what he called his "medicine." This was a concoction he'd made with fish and some type of shaving lotion that had been rotting in a jar for who knows how long. It didn't smell too good to me, but Dad said it attracted marten and fox for miles around.

Not far from the tent Dad began to set the first trap. Out of a partly-decayed log he found leaning on its stump, he chopped some short pieces which he split in half. He set three pieces on end in a row at the foot of a tree and another three pieces opposite the first ones, forming a passageway about four inches wide. The bait was placed at the far end, with the trap at the entrance, then the passageway was covered with boughs.

We didn't go as far as Dad wanted to that day because snow began to fall in big flakes. Dad figured we were in for a heavy snowfall and we didn't have our snowshoes with us. We ate our lunch and returned to camp. It snowed all night and by morning there was more than a foot of snow on the ground and it was still snowing, although the flakes were smaller. We spent the day sitting by the fire, but Dad was very restless. He walked around talking to himself; then he'd go and cut some firewood. I could hear him telling himself that now he'd have to raise the eight traps he had set earlier and reset them because they wouldn't catch anything under all that snow.

I woke up some time during the night when Dad got up to see if it was still snowing. He was happy that it wasn't and he said he was going to go alone in the morning to re-set the traps.

I was still in bed when Dad was ready to leave. "Don't get up," he said. "Stay in bed and have a good rest while you have the chance." But I wasn't one to stay in bed very long once I was awake. When I stepped outside, I could see that winter had come. The trees were loaded with snow; in fact, everything was white.

With the batter left in the bowl I fried a couple of crepes and drank a cup of black tea. Anxious to try my snowshoes, I put them on and walked around the tent. This was fun! Venturing out into the forest, I pretended to blaze trails and cut trees just like I would do on my own trap line. That kept me busy until just before dark, when Dad arrived. He was in a good mood and hurried to open his packsack and show me a marten. It was dark brown, with a pretty orange spot under its chin. It looked a little like a cat, but much smaller. As I was admiring the marten, Dad said, "You see, we've only been here for a short while and we have twenty dollars already. Give us a few weeks and we'll have well over a hundred dollar for sure."

I asked if he had set more traps and he had–four. "Now," he said, "we have one dozen traps set and if the weather holds, we should have three or four more martens by this time next week."

The more traps Dad set, the less I saw of him. Almost every day he left before dawn and didn't return until long after dark, always looking for better places to set traps or just exploring for a better place to go next year. He couldn't stand to spend even one day in camp, but always had to be on the move. These long days alone became very monotonous for me, so one day I said to him, "I don't know why you bothered to take me along. I seem to be more of a nuisance than anything else and it's not much fun for me to stay in the tent by myself every day waiting for you to come back."

Dad said, "If you think you can make it, you can come with me tomorrow. We'll try it for a day or two and if you can keep up, I'll start you a line of your own." We had been there for nearly a month and that was the best news I had heard.

The next morning I got up at the same time as Dad, gulped my breakfast, put on my snowshoes and waited for him to put the gear together. We left at daybreak, cutting a new trap line, with the traps about a mile apart. We kept this up for a long time, until I was so hungry I didn't think I could go any farther, but I didn't want to interrupt Dad's routine. Finally he said, "I guess we should stop and have something to eat; it must be close to lunch time."

He built a fire and brewed a pot of tea, using melted snow for water. As usual, he ate his lunch standing by the fire and that day I did, too, even though I was tired and very tempted to sit down. We set only one more trap that afternoon and then went back to camp. It was one of Dad's short runs, getting back when there was daylight left. He asked me if I as tired, but not willing to admit it, I said, "No. I could have gone a lot farther."

Dad said, "I feel a bit tired, but then I broke trail for you all day."

A week later Dad decided to start me on a trap line of my own. On this morning we left in the opposite direction of his lines and set traps until about lunch time. We set six traps and made it back to camp before sunset. At last I had something to do, so time went by much faster, and almost every day there was another marten to add to the pile of pelts. And each day meant we were another day closer to going home for Christmas.

The day I came back with the first marten from my own trap line I was so pleased I didn't want Dad to skin it that night. I wanted more time to just look at it, but Dad dressed it and put it on a mold. He had made several molds out of cedar slats that he would whittle during the evenings. The mold was shaped like the pelt and was designed to stretch the skin and give it a better chance to dry in the form of the animal. When the pelt was fastened to the mold to his satisfaction, Dad hung it up to dry.

We were sitting by the fire one evening when I said, "Dad, we should have brought a calendar with us. We don't know what date it is and we're going to miss Christmas."

"Oh no," Dad said. "I know exactly what date it is. Tomorrow is the fifteenth of December. We're going to leave here on the twenty-first, so we have five more days of trapping. You'd better hurry and catch a couple more marten!"

I shouldn't have asked what date it was because from that day on, time just dragged. It was so bad I couldn't stay in camp. I'd go around my trap line even if I didn't need to, just to kill time.

One day Dad came back earlier than usual and I asked if it was so that we could get ready to go home. "Well," he said, "kind of. I want to go and cut a few miles of trail to make it easier to get home. We have about sixteen miles to walk and it will be a lot faster going if we have a trail part of the way." I offered to do some cutting the next day but he said I didn't have to worry about it, he could do enough in the rest of that day to get us home.

Finally the day I had been waiting for arrived. Dad had prepared our lunch the night before, so we ate breakfast quickly and started down the trail. We had walked at least two hours before daylight arrived, and that was the end of the trail. From there on we were in dense forest, which slowed our pace considerably. We ate lunch long past noon, reluctant to waste any time. As soon as the remaining food was back in my packsack, we started out again and kept going at a fast pace until dark. That's when we came to the lake. I strained my eyes to see if I could spot our house, which was almost one-quarter mile from the lake, but I couldn't. Dad asked me if I was tired and I told him "No," even though I was nearly played out. My snowshoes felt awfully heavy, but I was too proud to complain.

When we got home, Mom had a nice meal on the table. She said, "I was expecting you tonight so I kept an eye on the lake. When I saw you on the ice, I prepared your supper. I was sure you'd both be starving."

I had barely finished eating when Mom pointed to a tub of hot water she had set up in a dark corner of the house. I was ordered to get in and have a bath, which I needed badly. Basking in the scalding hot water, I listened to Dad's voice over the crackling of the fire. He was saying to Mom, "You just don't know how lucky you are to have a man like me—a man who can go out and make big money. You see," he said, "the two of us in just over a month earned more than two hundred dollars. That's enough to pay the bill at the grocery store and have some left over to buy the kids some clothes."

Mom had to agree, and said she was willing to go along with him until they were back on their feet. After that, she expected him to find a steady job so he could be home every night. "I don't want to have to raise the kids and look after the farm alone," she said. "I want you to be a part of this family, too. It's just too much for me to handle."

I began to relax in the hot water. In fact, it felt so good that I fell asleep in the tub and didn't wake up until Dad picked me up to carry me to bed.

The next day Mom and Dad went to town, where Dad sold some furs. I was considered too young to go with them, but I knew how Dad got the best prices. Just before Christmas he took a couple of pelts to Bernard, the Jewish man who owned the dry goods store located across the street from the Hudson's Bay—a store Bernard disliked very much. Dad told Bernard he was selling these pelts in order to buy what his family needed until spring, and so they could have a nice Christmas. When he returned in the spring, he explained, he would have a large number of pelts and would sell them to Bernard if he could better the offer from the Hudson's Bay.

I knew that when Dad was finished trapping in the spring he would go to town with his packsack on his back. In town he would walk by Bernard's store once or twice, making sure Bernard spotted him, then cross the street and enter The Hudson's Bay. He would kill ten or fifteen minutes looking through a catalogue and fingering the merchandise, then cross over to Bernard's. Tossing his furs on the counter, Dad would tell Bernard that the Bay had offered him so much for this marten and so much for another, etc. Inevitably, Bernard would offer two to three dollars a pelt more, all the while telling Dad that the Bay was trying to rob him blind.

Meanwhile, Dad put some money on the grocery bill and brought back a big bag of apples and some candy. Mom bought a new pair of boots for Paul and a pair of pants for me. We had a terrific Christmas that year. After Christmas, Mom was busy canning moose meat for the summer, with Dad helping by cutting the meat while she added the seasoning and filled the large two-quart jars with the raw meat. When the jars were ready, they were placed in the canning pot to boil on the stove for hours.

By the time we had been home for ten days, Dad was restless, so we headed back to the trap line. Leaving at daybreak, we got to the tent before dark and the next day resumed the same out routine, except that I set more traps on my line. I kept asking Dad how to set traps for different animals and he was always happy to tell me. I wanted to catch a mink, so Dad showed me how to set my trap by a stream. Mink are fish eaters, whereas the marten hunted mice and squirrels. We looked for a place near the foot of some rapids where the water would stay open all winter. We set the trap among the rocks by a little cave and covered it with leaves.

So I tried my hand at setting mink traps and I guess I got lucky because I caught one and then a couple more marten before spring arrived and it was time to go home.

The second part of the winter seemed to go by fast, mostly because I was kept busy. I felt almost sad to leave, but Dad assured me we were going trapping again next winter–and we'd have it a lot better. "We are going to leave earlier," he said, "and build ourselves a nice warm cabin so we can spend the winter in comfort."

We were going to leave in the morning so Dad began to pack some of our belongings. "We have another two hundred dollars worth of furs," he said, "and that's enough to see us through the summer." It was still dark when we took the tent down. We finished packing and at first light we were on our way.

Dad was packing as big a load as he could, which made him sink deep into the snow with each step. I was right on his heels and he wasn't walking nearly as fast as I wanted him to; I was in such a hurry to get home. We ate lunch early because we happened to be near a creek where water was handy. Now, late in the afternoon and about three miles from the lake, we were both hungry. Dad took off his packsack, laid it on the snow, stretched, and said to me, "My friend, I know it's getting late and we're both hungry, but we're only a couple of hours from home. I sure would like to have supper at the table tonight. Do you think we can make it on empty stomachs?"

I was just as anxious as he was to get home, so I said, "We sure can, and I can take the big packsack the rest of the way if you want."

"No," Dad said, "I'll pack yours. I know you must be tired. I'm going to leave mine here and send Paul for it in the morning."

By the time we got to the house it was getting dark. Again, Mom was expecting us and supper was on the table. It was good to be back and have the rest of the family eager to hear about my trapping adventures.

Mom and Dad sold the furs the next day and paid the grocery bill and we each got one or two pieces of new clothing.

Mom said I needed to rest and she didn't want me to do any work for a few days, but I was so happy to be back I just couldn't sit still. I went to the barn to visit Bully and I think he recognized me when I scratched his neck because he rubbed his head on my chest. He was fat and healthy and seemed happy to see me.

When I got back to the house Mom was telling Dad that Paul hadn't had to cut a trail. She said that shortly after we had gone back after Christmas a surveyor and two men had cut a line for the construction of the road, which should start about mid-summer. "I served dinner to the men one day," she said, "and they each paid me thirty-five cents. Maybe when the road is completed I can open a café." But Dad was afraid people might think it was Mom who earned the living at our house. Whenever he didn't like one of Mom's ideas, he'd leave the room with a snort. And that's just what he did this time.

The snow was finally gone and the ground was beginning to thaw. We were ready to start working on the garden when Donat began complaining of stomach pains. Mom, after getting him to lie down with his knees up, down, and in different positions, decided he was having an appendicitis attack. Dad carried him to the little town of Senneterre, but there was no hospital there and they had missed the train, which came only every other day, so Dad carried Donat to Amos, a town forty miles away.

Donat's appendix was removed, and Dad stayed in Amos until he could take him home–by train this time. The rest of us sat on pins and needles for five long days, not knowing how Donat was faring.

By the time Dad got back, the garden had been spaded and we were waiting for warmer weather before doing the seeding. While we were waiting, Dad and Paul went to the far end of the farm looking for birch wood that Dad had seen some time before. While walking around, they heard sharp cries coming from a well-hidden hole in the hillside. There they found two baby foxes that had been abandoned by their mother. Dad brought them home and Mom force-fed them with condensed milk They soon regained their strength, growing quickly and becoming very nosey and mischievous. We called them Tibby and Farley. One of them chewed the top of Dad's leather boot and he got a licking. One day I was cleaning the stable when Farley joined me, but he kept jumping at the wall so I climbed on a box to see what it was he wanted so badly. There I found a jar that contained some of Dad's trapping medicine. I took the jar down and put it on the grass and Farley rolled the jar around and rubbed himself on it as if it were perfume. But these were wild animals and one morning when Dad had let the two of them out, as he did every morning, Tibby didn't come back. Farley stayed a little longer but he, too, was gone by fall.

Dad, Paul and I began burning the slash and pulling out stumps when Dad came down with appendicitis, too. He didn't wait for the pain to get too severe; he walked the forty miles to Amos again. He was ready to come home after five days, but he got pneumonia and had to stay in the hospital another week.

Mom, Paul and I worked from morning until night seeding and planting. When Dad came home from the hospital everything was done. Dad was ill most of that summer. He'd work in the field for awhile, then go back to the house to rest.

The three of us were in the field every day, clearing the land of stumps that were thick as hair on a dog's back. We'd pile them as high as we could, leave them to dry for a few days, then set fire to the piles. We worked hard all summer clearing land. We'd get so black from the fires sometimes we couldn't tell the colour of our clothes. Mom would quit work early and go to the lake to do a washing. When we'd see her come back Paul and I would go to the lake with Bully and wash him and ourselves.

After the evening meal Mom would stand on the back porch and watch the fires burning. If she saw a pile that wasn't burning well she'd go back to the field and stoke it, picking some of the smaller wood off the ground to feed it until it spouted a good flame. Some evenings she was in the field until dark.

For the whole month of July Mom and I worked alone because Dad and Paul were hauling hay from the priest's farm to feed Bully. By the beginning of August Dad figured we had about four acres of land cleared, which was enough, if seeded in hay, to feed Bully for the year. But Mom refused to quit, so she and I carried on with the clearing.

Dad began to dress some lumber to build a rowboat to get us to where the blueberries were plentiful and already in season. One Saturday afternoon Dad launched the boat, tested it, and pronounced it safe. The next morning we all got in except Paul, who chose to stay at home to look after Bully. We headed for the far end of the lake and Dad handed Mom a troll so she could fish on our way there. Mom loved to fish, and she got lucky; she caught a huge muskie. I had never seen Mom so happy. She sang all the rest of the way to where Dad said there were lots of blueberries just waiting to be picked.

As usual, Dad was right. We landed on a sandy beach and just a few feet into the forest there were blueberries as far as we could see. We picked until about noon, then went to the beach to eat lunch. But the water beckoned, so we all went for a swim, then sat on the sand and ate blueberry sandwiches. After resting in the sun for awhile, we went back to picking. We came home with boxes full of blueberries that Mom turned into jam and preserves the next day.

By the end of August Dad felt better and was able to help Paul and me cut firewood, re-chink the log house and take care of other chores that had to be done before winter.

One day we noticed smoke rising above the tree tops a few miles from the house. Dad went to investigate and saw a crew of men slashing and burning. He asked them what they were doing and was told they were building a railroad from Senneterre to Rouyn. One man told Dad there were a lot of gold mines opening in that area and the railroad was needed to service the mines.

Dad was jubilant when he related the news to Mom. "With so many mines opening up, there should be work for everyone, and miners earn big money. You may have your wish sooner than you expected; I might just go and get a job as a miner!"

Mom was happy to hear the good news, but she didn't agree with Dad going so far to find a job. Because the mines were a long way from home, he'd be away most of the time if he worked there. "You just wait," she said, "and something will open up around here one of these days. Then you can start looking." As far as the railroad was concerned, she was skeptical. "That's all very nice, but it doesn't give us a road to town and that's what we need badly right now. It's just like the government, to promise something and not follow through."

"Well," Dad said, "It's hardly worthwhile spending money on a road for one settler. But wait and see: as soon as more settlers move in, the government will have to build a road."

Around mid-October, Dad went hunting alone and came back in the afternoon with two moose livers. He had killed two moose again a couple of miles from the farm. I was setting the net every day to freeze fish for the winter and also catching a few rabbits to freeze. We had harvested a good crop of potatoes, carrots, onions, turnips and beets, so Dad and Paul dug a pit in the banks of the stream where the lean-to used to be and built a root house to keep the vegetables for the winter. Little by little we were becoming more self-sufficient.

We were working near the house one day when we were surprised to see a stranger emerging from the forest. He introduced himself as the Government Settlers' Agent in charge of monitoring the progress made every year by the settlers. He measured the land cleared during a one-year period and sent his report to the land agent. That agent, in turn, would remit a check for five dollars per acre for slashing and burning, and so much per acre for clearing the stumps and so on, until the land was at the stage of cultivation, to a maximum of five acres per year.

The settler's agent was amazed at the large area we had cleared in the short time we had been on the land. He said that a settler had to clear a minimum of five acres per year to honor his agreement. He would measure the land and send in his report as soon as he got back to his office. We could expect a check in the mail by the middle of December.

After measuring the land cleared, he reported that there were five acres in cultivation, so our check would be two hundred and fifty dollars. Before leaving, he explained that the subsidy had been set up as an incentive to move people out of the cities that had been so ravaged by the depression, and to encourage them to come to this area. He assured Mom that she would soon have neighbours because the construction of the road was slated to begin in the fall. Mom was much encouraged by the news.

Dad went to town one day and came back with four sides of salted pork, a bag of macaroni, a large amount of leaf tobacco for himself, and other items that were part of the winter storage supplies. He handed me a set of fleece wool underwear and said, "My friend, you're not going to freeze this winter!"

When I saw all that he had brought, especially the salted pork, I knew he was getting ready to leave for the bush again. He finally mentioned it a couple of days later. He was sitting by the lamp at the table, looking at a map. He asked me to come closer and pointed to a chain of large lakes. "You see here?" he asked. "We are going to go up this river and head up to this big lake, then we're going to cross it this way and about here we are going to build ourselves a nice cabin for the winter. It is situated so that, if we have to come out during the winter, we can walk out. It's about a thirty-five-mile walk and we can do that in one day if we have to. So, you had better get your snowshoes polished up and make sure they are in good shape because you are really going to need them this winter."

A couple of days later Dad began to fill small bags with beans, macaroni, a large bag with flour, and lots of tea and brown sugar, singing all the while.

CHAPTER IV

The rowboat had been loaded the previous afternoon, so we were able to leave with the first morning light. I was grateful for my fleece wool underwear because it was very cold. Dad's face took on a serious look as he concentrated on rowing with a steady stroke. He rowed in silence to the big island, followed its shores, then crossed over to what we kids called blueberry beach–the same beach where we'd had so much fun swimming and picking blueberries last August. I wished that month had never ended. Dad rowed slowly past the beach, still following the shoreline, and it seemed to me he was watching for some kind of marker.

About three miles past blueberry beach we came to a fairly large creek and Dad stopped rowing. He scanned the area for a moment, then resumed rowing for a short distance, when he stopped again. "We are going ashore here," he said. "I want to find the river I saw on the map."

I waited by the boat for almost an hour before Dad came back. "We are at the right place," he said. "I am going to take the axe and cut us a trail to the river, which is about a mile away. You can unload the boat and pack whatever you can up the hill and when I get back we'll drag up the boat. We're not going to have any trouble as the ground is level all the way."

I don't know how many trips I made to unload the boat and pack everything up that steep hill, but by the time I was finished I was really tired. I had just finished having a rest when Dad came back and said the trail was cut and we could portage to the river. The two of us pulled the boat up the steep hill, then Dad said he could handle the boat alone from there, while I packed whatever I could to the river. When I reached the river with my first load, I was disappointed. It didn't even look like a river. The water was green and slimy and there was no sign of a current. It looked more like a slough of dead water than a river.

I dropped my load and returned for another, meeting Dad on the way. He was placing rollers under the boat so it would move more easily. When he got the boat to the river, he rested for awhile and then we both made a few more trips to get the rest of the supplies. We reloaded the boat and Dad began to row again, but at a much slower stroke. I guess he was tired, too. I kept looking at the huge black poplars growing in the water on both sides of the river. The scene reminded me of something I had seen in fairytale books.

I found out later that the reason Dad was rowing so slowly was because he didn't know exactly where we were. But he knew there was an Indian village nearby and he didn't want to come upon it in broad daylight.

Gradually the colour of the water began to darken, making it look more like a river. When we came around a bend of the river, I noticed something very strange on the hillside: piles of stones and something that looked like racks built with poles, about six feet above the ground. Dad said it was an Indian cemetery so we must be getting close to the village.

From then on Dad was very careful not to make any noise with the oars and he told me to refrain from coughing. We went for a long time in silence, finally coming to a long, narrow body of water that looked like a lake. There was a strong wind coming from the far end and the waves were quite high. In a low voice, Dad said, "We are going to follow the shore here and try to get to the next bay where we'll stay until dark. I'll make us a bed and you better get some sleep, even if you're not tired, because we are going to have to travel under cover of darkness."

We bounced along on the waves, which were coming to us sideways, rocking the small boat. It took a long time to get to the bay but we made it safely. We landed on a rocky shore that was sheltered from the wind. Dad made us some lunch and then laid a tarp on the ground for me to lie on. Even though it was only late afternoon, I guess the lunch and the rocking of the boat had made me sleepy. At any rate, I didn't have any trouble going to sleep.

Dad woke me up during the night and said, "It's time to go." The wind had calmed down some but the waves were still high. We got into the boat again and Dad followed as closely to the shore as he dared, whispering to me, "Keep an eye out for a fire burning. If you see one, tell me."

I tried to watch the shore ahead, but everything was pitch dark. A dog began to bark near the beach and Dad rowed faster. The dog ran along the beach, barking at us, but I guess the wind carried the sound in a different direction so that no one heard. Not much later we rounded a point and headed up a narrow river that had a very strong current. Dad said, "By the look of things, we're not going to be able to go much farther tonight."

"Why not?" I asked.

"Because I wouldn't be surprised if there wasn't a waterfall or some rapids ahead."

"So what are we going to do?"

Well, if there is a waterfall, we'll just have to camp at the foot of it and wait until morning to have a good look. Then we'll decide what to do."

Dad was right. We traveled another couple of miles and as we rounded a bend of the river we heard the noise of a waterfall. Dad found a suitable place to land and we went ashore. While I cut some boughs to make us a bed, Dad slowly walked along the river in the dark to study the situation. When he came back, he reported, "It's not as bad as it sounds. It's only a small rapid so we'll be able to pull the boat up it fairly easily. We have nothing to worry about."

As cold as it was that night, Dad didn't build a fire. He was afraid that Indians might be traveling down the stream, shoot the rapids and see the fire or smell the smoke. We weren't very far from their village as the crow flies. We just covered up good and slept until morning.

Dad wanted to have a look at the rapids in the daylight, so I went with him. We walked along the edge of the river, Dad inspecting all the small details, and when we came to the head of the rapids he said, "We're not going to have any trouble. I'll pull the boat up with a rope and you, with a long pole, will walk along the shore and keep it away from the rocks. In no time we'll be at the head of it."

We went back and got the boat loaded and began to pull it along the shore. Dad had to walk in the water, which was sometimes well above his knees, while I stayed on the shore, pushing it away so it wouldn't beach. We made good progress, but by the time we reached the head of the rapids, Dad was soaked to the skin. He didn't have any choice; he had to light a fire and hang his wet clothes to dry, at the same time taking the opportunity to cook breakfast and brew a pot of tea.

I asked him why he didn't want the Indians to know where we were going.

"Well, the Indians don't like white men to trap for furs," he explained, "and if they find us, they might ravage our trap line. That's why I didn't want them to see us going past their village. They would have known for sure we were going trapping."

It was already getting late when we left the head of the rapids. Rowing against the current, which was still running fairly strong, was difficult, but we made good progress because Dad rowed as hard as he could. We rounded another bend and there again was that distinct noise of a rapid ahead. This time the noise was deafening. Dad rowed as near as he dared, then landed on a small sandy beach before we got into the swift current. He went ahead to assess the situation, while I stayed with the boat. He came back almost an hour later, looking happy.

"There's no way we can pull the boat up this one," he said. "It's a huge fall, but the lake is only about a mile from here and it won't be difficult to portage. You begin to unload while I cut a bit of a trail." After Dad cut the trail we toted everything to the lake, including the rowboat. We still had enough daylight left to make ourselves a good bed and we slept until dawn.

Dad lit a fire and cooked some crêpes for breakfast. This was our usual breakfast, although we treated ourselves to pork and beans once in awhile. I sat on a log near the fire and ate my crêpes the way I like them best, with brown sugar.

Dad studied the lake for a long time before deciding on which direction to go. Finally he said, "We're going to head kind of northeast; that way we'll be fairly close to shore. It's a big lake and with the load we have in this small boat we could find ourselves in trouble if a wind came up. So we'd better stay close to shore where we will have a chance to run for shelter."

Once in the boat, he rowed quickly and I could tell he wasn't sure where he was going. I asked him what the name of the lake was.

"I'm not sure," he said, "but I think this is Sifton Lake. It could be part of the chain I saw on the map." Then he added, "I should have asked your mother to read the name for me, but I guess it doesn't matter any, now we are here." After that, he seemed more confident, as if he had reassured himself that it really didn't matter.

He had been rowing for a long time when I told him I could see an island up ahead. He put the oars down and took time to load his pipe. "I'm getting hungry," he said. "Maybe we should pull in on that island and have some lunch." I told him I was getting hungry, too, so he headed for the island.

After lunch, Dad walked around the shoreline, investigating the area, as usual. When he came back he commented, "It looks to me like there's a very deep bay straight north of here. It's not that far out of our way and I think it's worth looking at. If it's what we want, we'll settle there for the winter."

I sat on a log beside Dad while he loaded his pipe. Suddenly we heard a noise a few yards away. Dad quickly put his pipe down on the log, tiptoed over to the boat and got his rifle. Without making a sound, he hurried up a small incline and disappeared from view. A few minutes later I heard a shot. I ran up the hill to find Dad looking at his kill.

"My friend," he said, "we have our meat for the winter. You cut some firewood and make us a bed for the night while I dress this moose."

It had been a long day, but both of us had a hard time getting to sleep. Moose calls came from every direction. Dad said, "We're really in moose country. It's too bad we're so far from home."

"How far?"

"I can't tell for sure, but probably around thirty miles or more."

Early next morning Dad began to chop logs for a cabin. He asked me to unload the boat and stack everything on the beach. That done, I looked around for something else to do. Dad didn't want my help with the cabin, so I took the troll and went fishing. After only a short time, I caught the biggest fish I had ever seen. Happy with my catch, I went back to show it to Dad and ask him what kind of fish it was.

"It's a muskellung," he said, "They look much like a northern pike, don't they? Why don't you go back and catch a few more? We can eat fish this winter, too, you know." So I spent most of the day fishing and caught a good supply to freeze for the winter.

By evening the walls of the cabin were up and half the roof was on, so we slept in the cabin that night. It wasn't very big, about twelve feet by ten, but it was much bigger than the tent and as much space as we needed.

There was frost every night now, and it wouldn't be long before the lake froze over.

Dad didn't want to use all the bread we had brought with us, so in the morning he mixed a batch of bannock and left me to bake it in the frying pan over the open fire while he went back to work on the cabin. By nightfall, the roof was on and he had split some cedar logs and made a door, a bed, and a small table.

I could see he was happy with his work. Setting the stove in once corner, he said, "All we have left to do is get us a good lot of firewood and chink the walls so we can keep the heat in, and we're set for a warm, comfortable winter." Then he added, "I'm going to let you do all of that while I start cutting some trails for my trap lines and set a few traps."

It took me about a week to place all of our belongings in the cabin, do the chinking and cut a small amount of firewood. By then the lake was frozen and we got a few inches of snow. Dad was away every day from early morning until dark, but it didn't bother me as much now to be left alone. I was getting used to it and would go out and cut firewood when I got too bored to stay in the cabin.

The weather had been extremely cold for the past eight or ten days and we didn't get any more snow, which made it hard to get around in the bush. Then it finally turned mild and we got a real snowstorm that kept us in the cabin for three days. When it was over, there was nearly two feet of snow on the ground. Then Dad was out again every day, coming back with a marten now and then, sitting on the bed and dressing his furs. He wasn't very talkative that winter; we seldom had a real conversation, which was kind of depressing for me.

One day I asked Dad if I could start myself a trap line across the bay that was less than a mile wide. "Why there?" he asked.

"Well, on that side of the lake I wouldn't interfere with your trap line and there should be some martens there, too."

"Go ahead as long as you blaze yourself a good trail and don't get lost. I can let you have eight traps; that should be enough for you this winter."

I left at the same time Dad did the next morning, packing a big lunch with me. I set out across the bay, but didn't go very far into the forest that day because the terrain was hilly and littered with windfall that made it very slow getting around. I set a couple of traps and stopped for lunch, making a fire so I could have tea. Remembering what Dad had taught me, I took off my snowshoes, placed them upright in a drift, and dug my moccasins well into the snow. This way, the heat from the fire wouldn't melt the snow on the moccasins, which would make them wet and cause them to freeze on my feet when I started on my way again.

The heat of the fire felt good, especially on my hands, which were getting cold. But the smoke caused my nose to run, which felt very uncomfortable.

I managed to set four traps that day, which turned out just fine because I took a different direction the next morning and set the other four traps, giving me two miles of trapline instead of one. That way I could go out twice a week, make the round of my traps, and still get back before dark. And with something to do twice a week, time would go much faster.

I tried to keep myself occupied so I wouldn't have time to think so much, but sometimes it just didn't work. Sometimes I didn't feel like sledding down the hill, but would just lie on the bed and think. I thought mostly about what I was going to do when I grew up, and one thing was for sure: I wasn't going to waste my time in the forest. I'd find a better way to earn a living. I wasn't about to sleep in my clothes every night for the rest of my life; I had made up my mind about that.

We were doing well for the short period of time we had been on this trip: three martens and two minks already–nearly as much as the previous winter's catch. I caught my first marten of the season, dressed it and put it on a mold all by myself. Dad teased me about it. "The reason you caught that marten is because it was tired of living and wanted to commit suicide; that's why it got into your trap!"

"If I had some of your medicine," I complained, "I would catch as many as you do, but you won't let me have any."

"If I had more, I'd give you some; but as it is, I might not have enough to last the winter."

Time was going by a lot faster than the winter before, probably because I was more interested in trapping now that I had my own lines, or maybe because it was so much nicer to be in a cabin instead of a tent.

One evening, out of the blue, Dad said, "Christmas is coming fast, my friend, and we are a long way from home with no trail to follow. It's going to be a long and miserable walk to get home this year."

I knew Dad was preparing me for one of his surprises, but I just asked, "How long is it before Christmas?"

"A little more than two weeks now," he said. "It would be nice to be able to spend it at home with the family, but it's such a long way to go I don't know if it's wise to try it. Maybe we should be smart and stay here until spring. But I am sure they are short of a lot of things at home, mostly clothes. It would sure be nice to go and sell the furs so they could buy what they need."

It was about ten days later that Dad dropped his bombshell. "If you don't mind staying here alone for a few days, I'll go home alone. I can make the trip in one day by myself and I would cut us a bit of a trail on my way back to make it easier for us to get out in the spring. Even just a few blazed trees here and there–just something to follow–would make the trip down a lot easier for us."

I guess I looked a bit dejected because he said, "If you come with me, we'd have to sleep at least one night on the way down and that wouldn't be too much fun, sleeping out in the cold. I don't mind if you decide to come; I'm just telling you this so you know what you're letting yourself in for."

I told Dad I'd stay and look after the cabin, but later on I remembered the awful week I had spent alone on the farm and I wondered if I had done the right thing. But this was another time and another place and besides, when I looked at Dad's happy face, I knew my decision was the right one. It wasn't as if Christmas was a big deal, anyway. We had never received what most kids would term 'real' presents–toys and such. Our gifts were usually badly-needed items of clothing like mitts or shoes. The one real present I had ever received–and I had never forgotten it–was a colourful little barn lantern filled with jelly beans that was given to me when I was about three and a half.

Dad was really happy to hear me say I was going to let him go alone. He said, "You're safe here, but don't take any chances; stay in the cabin. You won't regret this, I promise. In fact, I'm going to buy you a nice twenty-two rifle when we have money to spare, and you never can tell, there might be enough money left over this time after I sell these furs."

Dad didn't leave for two weeks, but the time went by like lightening. I wasn't looking forward to his leaving, even though he seemed sure he was going to bring back the rifle–and how I wanted that rifle! But, inevitably, the dreaded day came. Dad came back early one afternoon and announced he was leaving for home the next day. He began making preparations that same afternoon, counting the pelts: eight marten, five mink and a dozen weasels.

"Look at this," he said happily, "in less than two months we made over two hundred dollars. No one else I know can make that kind of money in such a short time."

When I got up the next morning, Dad was already at the stove cooking his breakfast while whistling between his teeth. In order to see, he had lighted the wick we kept in a can of moose suet we used as a candle. When he saw me, he told me to go back to bed. "There's no sense in you getting up this early. Go back to sleep."

But I stayed up, sitting on the edge of the bed watching him eat his meal standing at the table. He took a few sips of tea and was ready to leave, warning me not to go to my trapline. "Just stay around the cabin," he said. "That way you won't be asking for trouble."

I watched from the doorway as he headed north toward the end of the bay. It took a lot of courage to undertake such a long journey alone. I went back to bed, but couldn't sleep, just kept thinking about my dad and the long walk ahead of him. Then I began to get mad at myself for putting up a brave front when I was scared inside, and knew I was going to be lonesome.

Dad would be all right. He gave the appearance of a frail man, with a drawn look on his face, but he had tremendous energy and courage, and the endurance of a tiger. He seldom sat down, yet never seemed to get tired. His steely gray-blue eyes didn't seem to focus when he looked at you, but somehow he never missed nailing a moose at a dead run in the bush. He was of medium size–five foot eight–weighed about one hundred thirty-five pounds, was completely bald except for a line of hair above his ears and around the back of his head, and had very heavy eyebrows. He was a survivor of the 1919-20 typhoid fever epidemic. His hair had fallen off with the fever and it never grew back.

I felt better after a good night's sleep. Daylight brought a gray sky that looked like it might shed snow. Wanting the exercise so I would sleep that night, I went out and cut some firewood. The next day I woke early but just stayed in bed thinking about school. Why hadn't I brought some schoolbooks with me? I had plenty of time to read and improve my education. But, I thought, if I had mentioned it to Dad, he probably would have said, "You don't need any books and stuff. They would just add to the load we have to carry and we have enough as it is." Then he might have added, "I never went to school one day and I make more money than anyone I know who has spent half their lives in school."

I could have stayed in bed all day thinking of what might have been, but it wouldn't change anything, so I got up and cooked breakfast. There had been a bit of snowfall during the night so I put on my snowshoes and went for a walk. I walked to the far end of the bay and on my way back a moose came out of the bush and crossed a few hundred feet in front of me. Wishing I had my new rifle, I raised my arms, took aim and yelled: Bang! The moose was undisturbed by my antics.

On my fourth day alone I decided to make the rounds of my traps. My snowshoes were on, my lunch on my back and I was about to descend to the lake when I spotted five wolves chasing a moose across the bay at almost the same spot I had seen the moose a couple of days earlier. Even though he was running as fast as he could, I knew the moose didn't have a chance. The wolves were soon tearing at his sides and I saw one get on his back and bite his neck while another was biting at his nose. I watched helplessly until they disappeared into the forest on the other side, then I took off my snowshoes and went back to the cabin.

I didn't venture far from the cabin that day, but stayed close by, doing a few chores like packing in a good supply of wood and cleaning up the cabin–little jobs that didn't get done too often. I knew Dad would be back the next day, if not sooner, and he'd be pleased to find everything clean and in good order.

I mixed a batch of bannock, which I was getting pretty good at, and cooked a big pot full of moosemeat and macaroni so there would be something ready to eat when he arrived either that night or early the next day. And before darkness fell I made sure to get a bucket of fresh water. I went to bed early, feeling happy about having successfully tackled another difficult situation.

The sound of snowshoes on the crisp snow jerked me out of bed. I ran to the door and there was Dad, taking off his snowshoes. The first thing he said was, "I'm starving." He came in, dropped his packsack to the floor and helped himself to a plate of macaroni and moose meat.

The barrel of a rifle was sticking out of his packsack and without waiting for permission, I grabbed it. I couldn't believe it. My own rifle! Dad handed me two boxes of shells and my happiness was complete. I was so proud and excited I knew I wouldn't be able to sleep any more that night.

Dad laughed and said, "Look in the packsack. There's something else for you in there."

I dug further down and found two pairs of hand-knitted socks, a pair of woolen mitts and, at the very bottom, a bag of peppermint and a piece of cake.

Dad told me what was going on at home and in the surrounding area. Paul was still working on the road, digging ditches now, and spending a lot of his money on new clothes. But he would have to quit soon because the job was getting too far from home for him to get to work and back. He had slashed a huge area on the farm on weekends and the debris was piled up, ready for us to burn when it was dry. Rails were being laid for the railroad and a flag station and a house for the section foreman were going to be built about a mile from our place. There was talk of building a school near the flag station, too.

"Lots of activity going on everywhere," Dad said. "Your mother thinks I should apply for a steady job on the railroad, but I couldn't do that kind of work. It would just kill me to have to start and stop work at the sound of a whistle. A man would lose all his freedom." He shook his head in wonder that men would allow themselves to be trapped in such a way, much as he trapped the animals in the forest.

"We are much better off doing what we're doing now. At least we have nobody pushing us around. If we don't feel like going out one day, we don't go, and we still make the same money as long as the traps are set properly."

Mom was going to have a hard time getting Dad to settle into a steady job. He loved the freedom of the wilderness too much to give it up.

We resumed trapping until the end of March. The snow was just perfect; in fact, it had been a really good winter. The weather had remained in the minus forties, which kept the marten active, so we left for home with plenty of furs.

The farm had changed a lot. Paul had slashed a long strip at the front, and with the forest being pushed farther from the house there would be fewer mosquitoes. We could see men working on the railroad and Mom was looking forward to having neighbours to talk to rather than living in isolation. As well, there was talk of mines opening up a few miles south of our place, which would bring in passers-by and increase traffic on the road. And the nicest part of all: we wouldn't have to raft across the lake to get to town.

The following January, Paul had to quit his job. He tried to get one on the railroad, but didn't succeed. He was thinking of leaving as soon as the snow was gone, to try his luck in a gold mine. That made me very envious. He was so lucky to be fifteen, I thought. He had showed me all the clothes he'd bought, which hadn't cheered me up any, and now he was talking of all the things he was going to do when he started to earn big money working in a gold mine. It was all very depressing.

Mom seemed to be encouraging Paul in all his plans. She mentioned that he had given her some money to buy a dress but she had bought material instead, to make it herself. She went to her bedroom and proudly brought out the material to show me. This was absolutely the last straw! I figured, *One of these days I'm going to be fifteen, too. Just you wait and see!*

I had to get out of the house so I paid Bully a visit. On my way back I saw Mom and Dad outside, talking. Mom was telling Dad where she wanted him to build a chicken coop and Dad was saying he would start on it as soon as the snow was gone. Things were back to normal and I knew that before long Mom would ask me to get busy and clear some more land.

For some reason I didn't feel like working on the farm that spring. I didn't feel like doing anything at all. In fact, I always felt tired; even getting out of my chair was an effort. Perhaps it was caused by an inner resentment toward Paul for being so much older and able to do the things he wanted to do. He could walk to town and see a movie, or even play some pool. He'd come back late at night and wake me up to tell me all the fun he'd had. All that did was feed the resentment I already felt. I was considered too young to go to town by myself; there were evil things going on in town which kids my age shouldn't know about.

Whenever Mom asked me to do something, I'd always try to put it off until later. Mom would get exasperated with me and sometimes, after asking me three or four times, she'd get really mad and say, "Son, when are you going to get out of your cocoon and do what I asked you to do an hour ago?"

I don't know why, but it made me mad when she used the word "cocoon." It sounded as if she meant I was something out of this world. One day I asked her why she always said that to me. "I don't think it's a very nice thing to say, and I don't like it."

Mom didn't have as much patience as Dad, but sometimes she would take the time to explain and she did that day. I think she knew I was a bit jealous of Paul.

"You know what a cocoon is, don't you?" she asked.

"Yes, it's one of those wormy things we find hanging in small bushes, with an egg all wrapped in a kind of silky stuff."

"Exactly. And the egg grows inside the cocoon and when it reaches a certain stage it comes out of the cocoon and grows a set of wings. It becomes a butterfly and flies away. Well, kids growing up are just like that. But it takes kids a lot longer to fly on their own and they have parents to guide them along the way–to teach them. They have to learn their responsibilities in life from their parents so they can become able to take care of themselves as well as others."

Mom's talk didn't sink in very deeply at that time, but thinking about it over the next couple of weeks I came to realize that I just had to wait for another four or five years for my wings to grow enough to fly away. Meanwhile, I tried to do whatever Mom asked me, no matter how tired I felt.

We began burning the slash and cleaning between the stumps. Before we were finished, Dad and Paul started building the chicken house while I kept up with the burning.

The road was barely dry when settlers began to move in. Almost every day there were people stopping by the house for something to eat, and they would take time to visit and ask questions about the area.

Mom bought a dozen chickens and a big red rooster. Next she bought a cow, and Dad was talking about getting a horse and retiring old Bully. It gave me a renewed interest in the farm because I figured we were becoming big farmers now, with chickens, a cow and, especially, a horse. The horse would make it so much easier to clear the land.

Paul didn't stay home for very long after the chicken house was completed. He came back from town one afternoon and announced that he and his friend could get a ride on the freight and were going to Val-d'Or to look for jobs in one of the many gold mines already in operation there. He packed his clothes and was gone a few days later.

About mid-summer, Dad bought a horse and decided to sell Bully to one of the settlers because it would take too much hay to feed three animals through the winter. I felt sad that we had to get rid of Bully. He had been a good friend to me, someone I could talk to when I had no one else to unload my troubles on. But he wasn't going to be far from our place so I could visit him now and then.

Dad didn't stay home very long that summer. He found a job and was away until the middle of August. When he got back he got busy building a rowboat that we used a couple of times to go picking blueberries and to set the fishing net.

Mom and Dad had moved their arguing headquarters to the chicken house, and of late they had been having very long "discussions" there. A few times Mom returned to the house very disgruntled, going as far as to say she was ready to pack her bags and go live with one of her sisters. We all knew she was desperate about something, but we didn't know exactly what. Gemma, Noella and I would meet behind the barn to plan what we would do if Mom carried out her threat to leave the farm, but we never could come to an agreement. Gemma said Mom would have to take all the kids with her, except me; I'd have to stay with Dad and start trapping on my own to earn money to support them. I wasn't in favour of that. If they were all going with Mom, then I was going with them and that's all there was to it.

Things didn't go that far. Whatever the problem, Mom eventually consented to whatever Dad wanted to do.

With things back to normal, Mom decided to take me in hand. "You know," she said, "you're not very friendly. You need to go out and find someone to talk to. The neighbour says you go right by their door when you visit Bully in their barn, and you don't even drop in to say 'hello' to them. You can't do these kinds of things. You have to talk to people and act civilized."

I guess she was right, but I was very shy and didn't like to meet people. I felt I didn't have anything to talk about. I could answer questions, but to start a conversation was impossible. I wasn't used to conversation anyway, because Dad and I never had that much to say to one another in the bush and I didn't know anything about the outside world. But one day, at Mom's insistence, I went to see the new flag station and section foreman's house. Walking slowly down the road, I tried to think of what to say if I met somebody at the station, but I couldn't come up with anything that made sense. My worries were soon over, however, when I found that what was hard for me was easy for other people.

After slowly climbing the two steps to the station platform, I stood for a moment, afraid to advance any farther. But my footsteps had been heard by the men inside, and one of them came out to greet me.

"My name is David," he said. "Come on in. Where do you live?"

"On the farm nearest the lake."

"Oh, you must be the trapper's boy."

I nodded my head up and down as he continued. "You have been trapping for several winters, haven't you? Do you like it?"

He asked me many questions before telling me that he had a boy about my age. I asked him where his boy was and he said, "He's at boarding school now and he won't be home until Christmas. It's too bad you didn't come by a couple of weeks sooner; you would have met him. Now you won't see him until school is out at the end of June."

I cut my visit short before I ran out of things to say, but I knew David liked me and he would be a good friend to have To my surprise, he had been easy to talk to and not at all what I expected from a stranger.

I told Mom about David and she said she had met him. "He came here to buy eggs a few times," she said. "He's a very nice man. He wants me to visit with his wife and I'd really like to, but it seems I never have the time. Maybe one of these days I'll forget about the work here and just go."

And maybe, I thought, I'll try to forget about my shyness and meet some more people. It hadn't been so difficult, after all.

CHAPTER V

When fall arrived Dad began once again to put the trapping gear together, this time with more and better equipment: a better stove, lots of new traps, and more groceries than we had ever taken with us. Another new addition was a dog named Puce. She was a small black Lab that someone had given to Paul, but with Paul gone Dad decided to take her along with us as company for me around the camp.

Dad was at his happiest in the fall. In fact, he was a different man entirely, singing all day long, and not able to sit still for any length of time. He had to be up and about, always doing something. Last year, before we headed out, he had spent a lot of time studying the map and retaining in his mind the names of all the lakes we were going to have to cross. This time he knew exactly where he wanted to go and was anxious to get started.

We set out a couple of weeks earlier than we had last fall, following the same river system. Once again we waited until dark to pass the Indian village, sleeping at the very same spot as before. We slept on the shore of Sifton Lake the next night, heading in a different direction in the morning. We had to hunt in a new area each year; otherwise the game became too sparse. We headed southeast, following the shoreline.

Dad was so happy he was almost smiling when he began to sing another one of his funny little songs that most of the time included one of us kids. This time it was about me:

Once my friend
Built himself a sailboat.
Once my friend
Built himself a sailboat.
He knew not how to sail
So he kept it on the shore.

He had a beautiful tenor voice that would have put Caruso to shame, but he was much too shy to sing in public, where I am sure he could have earned a better living than by trapping.

There was always a bit of teasing in the songs Dad made up for us, but I enjoyed his singing immensely, even if it was me he was teasing this time. I was relaxed, watching the scenery go by: giant cedars leaning toward the water, sending their fragrance into the air. We passed near the mouth of a small, gently-flowing stream where two moose stood up to their bellies in the water, pulling lily pad roots up from the bottom to eat. And once in awhile I'd look up to see a flock of geese migrating south. I was enjoying every mile of our trip, surrounded by so much beauty that I didn't really care how far we were going or how cold it was getting.

Toward the middle of the afternoon Dad handed me the troll so I could catch a fish for supper that night, and before long we had a nice big muskie in the boat.

With Dad rowing at the same steady speed, we went a long way that day, stopping for the night at a long, sandy point covered with thick green moss and shaded by tall pine trees. We came to a river the next morning, rowed up it for about a mile and arrived at a small lake. There had obviously been people there at one time because there was a landing dock to tie up planes and a place of encampment farther from shore.

We crossed the lake and continued up the river until we came to a very large lake that was almost round and had one small island near the shore. Dad decided we should cross the lake as it was the middle of the afternoon and unlikely that a wind would come up. He rowed quite fast because the lake was about ten miles across and he wanted to get to the other side safely. Even so, it was dark by the time we landed on a stony beach and pulled the boat ashore.

As he was lighting a fire, Dad said, "My friend, we have just crossed the Machimanitou Lake; that's what the Indians call it. It means 'the lake of the evil spirit' because it can get pretty rough in a wind storm and probably a lot of Indians have drowned crossing it." He looked around and shook his head. "Too bad there's no shelter anywhere near the lake. It would be a good place to spend the winter."

Next morning we had loaded up the boat and followed the shoreline for a couple of miles when we came to a river. Dad rowed up the river for a few miles and at a spot where it widened a little we landed on a nice sandy beach. As usual, Dad scouted the area and when he returned he said, "We are going to build ourselves a cabin and spend the winter here. It looks good to me."

By the beginning of March, Dad realized he had picked a really bad area for trapping. Even if all the good signs were there, the marten weren't. In fact, it was the worst place Dad had ever chosen. There were no moose, no rabbits, not even grouse. It was a good thing we had taken so many more supplies than usual with us or we would have had to leave long before our regular time. On the other hand, we may have been better off to have run out of food and leave early because spring came three weeks ahead of time.

We woke up to a light drizzle one morning, thinking it was going to last only a few hours, but it drizzled all day and all night. By mid-morning the snow was getting soft and disappearing fast and by the next afternoon Dad began to worry that the weather might stay mild. He was right to worry. The drizzle that had changed to a light rain continued to come down until the snow was almost all gone. We were going to have trouble getting back home.

It took us two days to raise the traps and by that time we could see patches of moss here and there, hardly enough to get through with the sleigh. We left camp long before daylight, with the rain coming down on us, and before long we were soaked to the bone. Dad was helping the dog pull the sleigh with a top line and I was pushing behind with a pole.

We didn't get very far that day. We spent the night under a shelter of boughs with a fire nearby, trying to dry ourselves a bit We didn't get much sleep that night. Dad didn't know for sure where we were, but he thought we were fairly close to Sifton Lake and that we should reach it by mid-morning. He wasn't far off; we got there about lunchtime. We both stood and looked at the lake, which had at least a foot of water on top of the ice. Beyond the lake there was no snow left in the bush and we were still more than forty miles from home.

After eating lunch, Dad told me to carry on across the lake with Puce and the sleigh. He pointed in the direction he wanted me to go and said he would catch up to me later. He had noticed a large birch a couple of miles back. He was going to get the bark off the tree and build a canoe, as it seemed to him that was the best way for us to make it home with our gear.

I began to cross the lake with Puce. She was so small she almost had to swim where the ice had sunk under the heavy load of water on top of it, but she didn't have to pull the sleigh; I was doing it for her. After wading the eight or nine miles to the other side, and hoping I was at the place Dad wanted me, I climbed the embankment and set my packsack down under a white spruce. I rested a while, then lighted a fire to dry my clothes and to signal Dad so he could find me. It was almost dark when he arrived with a roll of birch bark tied on top of his packsack. I had supper ready and we ate standing by the fire, drying ourselves.

We slept under the boughs of the white spruce that night, and the next day, while Dad prepared the ground to start work on the canoe, I made us a shelter with boughs and moss. It rained for another two days.

There were no cedar trees anywhere near and Dad needed the cedar for the canoe frame, so I went searching. After walking in all that slush, I did find some and dragged two logs back t camp. I kept dragging in more logs as Dad dug in the frozen ground to shape a mold for the canoe. The next day I went ever farther in search of cedar and near the end of the bay I began to find dead muskrats floating on top of the water. I brought half a dozen of them back to camp and showed them to Dad. He said the water had risen too fast and the muskrats had drowned in their lodges. I skinned them and put the hides on molds, saving the meat to eat. By then our food supply was getting low and we had to save the flour to feed Puce as she refused to eat muskrat.

Dad began work on the canoe. He placed the birch bark on the ground he had prepared, laid down a frame pointed at both ends, loaded it with rocks to keep the shape and slowly folded the bark to the contour of the frame. He used hot water to help bend the bark, and drove stakes into the ground to hold it in place. After a couple of days the canoe began to take shape. Dad had found a large root with the proper curve to use at each end of the canoe. He split the root in half, then hewed it into the shape he wanted. He then began to tack on the frame along the edges, starting in the middle and working toward each end. I was amazed at the speed and deftness with which he worked.

With the canoe near completion, Dad asked me to make a notch in a jack pine tree and light a fire at the base to draw out some pitch that he needed to seal the seams, with the help of some canvas strips. After a few hours of burning a low fire at the base of the tree, the pitch began to drip into the can and soon there was enough. Dad mixed a bit of lard with it and sealed three of the seams. In less than two weeks, we had a sea-worthy canoe.

While the ice had melted along the edge of the bay where the sun created the most heat, the rest of the lake was still under three feet of ice. At least we could use the canoe to set muskrat traps while waiting for the rest of the ice to melt. But it took nearly two weeks for the lake to clear and by then we were out of flour. We caught a few fish, but Puce didn't eat fish. She hadn't eaten for two days.

It was still dark one morning when I awoke to the sound of a rifle. Dad had heard a noise nearby, saw it was a young bull moose and shot it. We all had a good feed of moose liver for breakfast.

When the ice had melted and it was time to leave, we found we had a lot more than the small canoe could hold. Dad wasn't about to leave the moose meat behind so he left some of our less expensive gear instead. We followed the shoreline and made it to the portage where we had slept twice before, arriving early in the afternoon. Dad made a couple of trips across the portage while I prepared a place for us to sleep. Long before daylight next morning we were up and began our last trip across the portage and down the river, portaging again at the rapids near the Indian village.

As we rounded the point and came to the village Dad kept away from the shore, but the chief saw us and hollered to us. Dad ignored his call until the chief fired a shot into the air, then Dad pulled in at the pier. The chief greeted us with a friendly smile and a Kwe Kwe salutation. He could speak a few words of English and Dad a few words of his language. The Indians, who were poor at both trapping and fishing, were always curious about where we had been and how successful a winter we had had. Dad told the chief we had been trapping and we'd had a very poor winter. The chief smiled, nodded his head, and waved for us to leave.

We spent the night at the head of the slimy Green River and portaged the next morning, arriving home that afternoon. Mom had been worried sick for nearly a month and was about to ask for a search party to look for us, so she was very happy to have us arrive safe and sound.

A school was under construction and was slated to open in the fall. Noella and Donat were going to attend, but Gemma and I wouldn't be going. We felt we were too big now to sit with nine-year-old kids.

Paul was still working at the mine, but came to visit now and then. There was a lot of traffic on the road, which was almost completed as far as Val-d'Or. We even had mail delivery and bus service.

That summer of 1939 went by so fast I didn't have time to see it. Mom and I cleared a lot of land while Dad was away working at some jobs. Mom still worked until dark a lot of the time, stoking the fires. For a woman her size, I don't know where she got all her strength and endurance. She was very tiny–barely five foot tall–but quick on her feet. She had a sharp, commanding voice and when she said something, she meant it. I guess that's why she didn't have any trouble keeping all of us under control. And she could remedy a situation immediately, like the morning she woke up to the sound of the chickens squawking wildly. She got up to investigate, found that Puce had broken through the chicken wire fence, gotten into the coop and killed five chickens. We all woke up to the sound of the rifle. Mom was so mad that she shot Puce then and there. There was no way she was going to have a chicken-killer on the farm.

By the fall of 1940, the war had been raging for a year. Mom and Dad never missed listening to the news on the radio (a new addition to our household). Mom was worried for Paul, who was old enough to be called up. She'd say, "We just got through a depression, a time when there was no money to go around to feed the hungry people and now they have millions of dollars to fight a war. I don't see why people can't live in harmony on this God-given earth."

Dad and I left for the trapline again that fall, one week after my fifteenth birthday. We had two dogs with us this time that were well trained to the harness. They had been given to Dad by a family that was moving to a mining town and couldn't take the dogs along. We also had a much bigger rowboat that was packed full of supplies. By now I had resigned myself to trapping with Dad until he was too old to do it any more. I just didn't see a way out for me.

We headed out over the same route as last time, with me sitting in the back of the boat, the two dogs at my feet. Dad rowed right past the cabin we had stayed at the previous winter; he seemed to want to go farther and farther every year. We didn't have to go a hundred miles into the bush to find marten; we could have trapped a lot closer to home. I didn't think it was fair, but Dad was the boss and I didn't have much to say in the matter.

About five miles past our old cabin we got into the Marquis River, which was very narrow and winding. Willows grew on both sides, almost blocking the passage at times and making it very difficult to navigate. We had traveled up the river for about ten miles when we came to a small lake about a mile long and half a mile wide. Dad was happy to see the last of the Marquis.

Long before we got there, Dad spotted the place where we were to spend the winter. "We're going to head for that point on our left," he said, "and build ourselves a cabin."

His mind made up, Dad didn't bother to scout the area for marten. Evidently we had gone far enough; eighty miles or more was a long way to walk home. We built a cabin and got half a dozen lines going and before long we were catching a lot of marten, mink, and even otters and weasels.

By the middle of March, Dad was ready to go home. "We have enough furs," he said. "We're going to let the population replenish itself so we have some to catch next year."

Dad built a good sleigh, which we packed the night before we left, leaning the sleigh against a tree so the snow wouldn't freeze on the runners. We left long before dawn, Dad walking ahead, cutting a trail as he went. I followed behind with the dogs. Sometimes I was close enough to hear Dad talking to himself, a habit I guess he had picked up from being alone so much in the bush.

We didn't go very far before the dogs began to tire, so Dad slowed the pace somewhat. Not having been harnessed for the past four months or more, they had no endurance. We got to Machimanitou Lake after dark and ate supper there. Dad was restless and wanted to get going again, but I talked him into resting the dogs a bit longer. Actually, I was getting tired myself as I had been packing the trail for the dogs, so it hadn't been an easy walk. I could feel my snowshoes getting heavy on my feet and I told Dad so.

"It's going to be a lot easier on the lake," he said, "where the wind has packed the snow, so you won't have to do that. The dogs won't sink so much, either. It's not going to take us long to cross the lake."

As we got on the lake I noticed a pale half moon hanging overhead in the hazy sky. But I didn't have much time to gaze around; Dad was walking much faster than he had been and we were soon lagging a long way behind him. I deliberately kept a slower pace because I didn't want to rush the dogs; nevertheless, I knew they wouldn't be able to go much farther.

About the middle of the lake Dad stopped to wait for us and he tried to slow the pace when we got going again, but gradually increased it unknowingly. I got the top line out, tied it to the lead dog, and began helping them pull the sleigh. We were moving very slowly because the dogs were tired and so was I. Dad, however, seemed to have the same energy as when we started out that morning.

All I could see ahead of us was a bluish line that was the far shore of the lake, and the moon that kept getting lower and lower in the sky. I could hear the howling of the wolves in the far distance, which didn't make me feel any better, either. I tried not to look ahead, because every time I did it seemed we weren't getting any nearer the shore. I felt as though I were a hundred years old and had crossed that lake a thousand times and would have to cross it year after year for the rest of my life.

In the middle of contemplating a change in my future, I heard Smoky let out a yelp. I stopped to see what was wrong and discovered a large blister on one of his shoulders. I called out to Dad, who came back to have a look. He patted Smoky's shoulder and told me to lead the way, pointing out the direction to go, and he took my place pulling the sleigh with the top line.

We came to the other side of the lake just as the moon was beginning to disappear. Before we were in complete darkness, we hurried to make camp. I stacked a big pile of boughs on the ground while Dad built a fire. I took the harness off the dogs and gave them some food, but they were too tired to eat. Dad made supper and after eating I lay on the bed, watching Dad sitting by the fire, smoking his pipe and drinking tea–talking to himself all the time.

It was a cold night and I was glad when the dogs came and lay on the bed beside me, keeping me warm. It was so cold we could hear the bark breaking on the trees, making a sound like rifle shots.

Dad went straight to sleep as soon as he lay down, but I was too tired to sleep; I needed to relax a bit first. I got up to put a log on the fire and spotted a wolf just a few feet away. My rifle was on the sleigh, but I saw Dad's thirty Winchester where he had stuck it in the snow just a couple of feet from where I stood. I made a grab for it and took a quick shot. To my great surprise, the wolf fell dead.

Dad woke up with a start and asked what was going on. I told him I'd just shot a wolf.

"I knew earlier we were surrounded by a pack of six or seven wolves," he said, "but I didn't want to tell you in case you would worry and wouldn't be able to go to sleep. We'll be fine now for the rest of the night. The pack will move on and leave us to sleep in peace."

Dad went right back to sleep, but I was awake for a long time, listening to the wolves howling a short distance away. I might have slept for two hours when Dad woke me up to tell me breakfast was ready. When I got up all the joints in my body ached; my legs felt heavy as lead, not rested enough from the long, hard walk. I looked at the dogs who were lying on the snow and neither of them moved as much as a muscle when I called them, but at least they had eaten their food sometime during the night.

Dad padded Smoky's collar and cut a hole in it where his blister was so it wouldn't be irritated further. Then we harnessed the two of them and were on our way. We walked for at least two hours in the dark. When daylight came, we made much better time. Dad walked ahead cutting trail and I followed with the dogs, tramping the snow down again so they wouldn't sink too deeply and get tired too early in the day.

It was well past noon and Dad showed no evidence of stopping when I finally said I was starving. He said, "I'm getting hungry, too, but I thought we might try to get to Fish Lake and eat there. We'll only be about twenty miles from home and I was hoping to get there by early evening, but I guess we won't be able to make it."

I told him: "I can't go another mile before eating, and we have to give the dogs a rest. Rover seems fine, but Smoky is very tired; he's just about ready to drop. They need to rest if we want them to get the sleigh home."

We walked a bit farther until Dad found a spot he liked. He built a fire, melted some snow for tea water and we had a good lunch. Dad didn't rest; he hardly sat for two minutes. He just kept walking around the fire talking to himself, holding a cup of tea in one hand and his pipe in the other. Finally, he said, "We had better get going. We don't have much daylight left and we're still a fairly long way from Fish Lake."

It was dark when we got to the lake. We crossed it and got into the bush again. I tied the top line to the lead dog and began to pull the sleigh with them as I could see they were both tired out. Their tongues were hanging out, almost dragging in the snow, and we were barely making any headway. After a couple of miles Dad, who was a long way ahead of us, waited along the trail and took my place pulling the sleigh. This didn't last very long because I couldn't lead the way in the dark. I didn't know in what direction to go and kept wandering off the trail. Dad took the lead again and I went back to help the dogs pull the sleigh. But it wasn't long before Smoky lay down and refused to move. I called Dad and he came back, took one look at the dogs and said, "They can't go any farther. They're completely tired out. We're going to take their harness off and leave them here with some food. When they're well rested, they'll find their way home."

Dad pulled the sleigh while I pushed behind with a pole, but we didn't move very fast in the soft snow. Arriving at Lake Tiblemont late at night, we sat on the shore and rested for a long time. Still exhausted, we began our trek across the lake, leaving the sleigh at the edge of the bush where we would retrieve it the next day. It was only a two-mile crossing, but it seemed like ten to me, and the last quarter of a mile was the worst. I kept looking at the house in the distance and it didn't seem to get any nearer. Of course, we were walking more slowly by now; even Dad had slowed down. I'm sure he was just as tired as I was, but he was too proud to admit it.

We arrived at the house around three in the morning and I was so happy to be back. As we were taking off our snowshoes outside, Dad said, "I knew you would make it. You're getting to be a good trapper and a good trapper always has to reach his destination if he wants to survive."

We came in just as Mom was lighting the lamp. She had heard us talking and had gotten up in a hurry, sure that we would be hungry. She stoked the fire in the stove and put some water on to heat. I sat on the first chair I saw near the door and thought I would never be able to get out of it again. My legs began to cramp so badly I couldn't move; I was in agony. Dad pulled off my boots and rubbed my legs. When the cramps began to ease, he got me out of the chair and helped me walk back and forth until the cramps were gone.

After we had eaten, Mom said, "You two smell like the barn. You'll just have to have a bath before going to bed."

"What do you expect us to smell like?" Dad protested. "We've been sleeping in the same clothes we were wearing when we left five months ago."

I got into the tub first and really enjoyed the luxury of a nice, hot bath. Afterwards I put on a clean suit of underwear and was ready for bed.

When I got up the next day I was alone in the house, and no wonder–I had slept until 1:15! While I was dressing I looked through the window and saw that Dad had pulled the sleigh up from the lake, but it was sitting there with most of the load still on it. Later I checked the barn and the horse and the other sleigh were gone, so I knew they had gone to town.

I had just finished a heaping plate of pork and beans when I saw Rover coming up from the lake, with Smoky following a half a mile behind. When they arrived at the house I let them in and gave them fresh water and food, praising them for the good job they had done finding their way home.

Mom and Dad came back about 4:30, along with Noella and Donat whom they had picked up from school. Roland was with them, too. He was not quite six so he wasn't in school yet, but he was getting to be a big boy. It was nice to see everybody again. I asked Mom where Gemma was. Mom said she was working as a housekeeper for an elderly couple and didn't have a chance to come home very often. Paul had quit his job at the mine and was now driving a bus for another mine. She said he was happy on his new job.

Dad finally told me why they had gone to town early that morning. "My friend," he said, "we are going to build ourselves a new house." He explained that the log house had been built too close to the highway and had to be removed.

"We had to sign some papers agreeing to sell the house and the right of way to the department of highways," he said, "and we will receive a check for six hundred dollars for it all!"

Dad made a deal to exchange logs for lumber with one of our neighbours who had set up a small sawmill and had quite a pile of lumber stacked in his yard. With the help of another neighbor, Dad began to dig a basement in three feet of frozen ground, while I cut logs and hauled them to the sawmill, returning with a load of lumber.

By the end of May we were able to move into our new home. It was a small house, built of rough lumber, but was still a big improvement over the log house. This one had a large bedroom downstairs and three small bedrooms upstairs.

Dad was in a big rush to look for work that spring, so he let Mom and me do the garden and all the seeding while he headed out with the two neighbours who had helped him with the house. They were going to try for jobs in a gold mine that had just begun operations a few miles away. Mom was really happy when Dad and his friends found steady jobs in the mine. Now Dad could come home on weekends and help with the farm work.

When the seeding was done Mom and I began to clear land again to add to the nearly thirty acres already under cultivation.

One day while we were working, Mom said, "I wish I could be sure your dad was going to stay on that job. It would make me feel so happy and secure." She shook her head. "But he's had many good jobs since we've been married and as soon as fall comes he gets that trapping fever and there is nothing I can do or say to make him stay at his job. He just packs his gear and is off to the wilderness and it seems the farther he goes, the better he likes it."

She stopped work and stretched her back, and there was a hopelessness in her voice when she continued, "I don't know how much more I can take of this; with this farm getting bigger every year I won't be able to look after it alone. I don't know what I'm going to do."

Mom's uncertainty upset me. I didn't know what she might do, and not knowing the future was always hard on me. I felt sorry for Mom, too. I knew she was working as hard as any man–even harder than most–to build a farm, hoping against all odds that one day Dad would give up trapping and develop an interest in the farm. Sometimes I lay awake half the night wondering how I could help.

One day I said, "Mom, maybe I should tell Dad I don't want to go trapping with him any more because there's too much work for you here on the farm and you need my help more than he does."

She told me she appreciated my concern, but nothing could change my dad from doing what he liked best. "He would venture out into the bush alone," she said. "I'm sure of that, and that would be a bigger worry to me than looking after the farm by myself. Knowing that he was a hundred miles into the bush, all alone, with his health not good, I'd worry about him getting sick or shooting himself by accident. No, we'll just wait and see what happens. Time has a way of arranging everything, and I'm sure it will all work out for the best when the time comes."

Mother had a way of making things work out her way nearly all the time. A few days after our conversation, she came back from visiting the next door neighbor and she had a radiant smile on her face. I knew something good had happened and it wasn't long before she told me.

"The neighbor wants his five acres of land plowed so he can apply for his grant this fall and I told him you would plow his land if he wanted to trade some of his time this winter helping with the chores I can't handle, and he agreed." The hopelessness of a few days ago was gone from her face. "This is going to put my mind at rest a little," she continued. "If your dad decides to go trapping, I know now I can get some help. Monday morning you can start plowing his land. It's all black soil, so one horse can pull the plow easy and it shouldn't take you much more than a week to do the whole five acres. If you can do that, it would be the biggest favour you will have done me this summer."

I assured Mom I would get started at first light Monday morning.

CHAPTER VI

I had kept up my friendship with Dave, the section foreman, and every so often I'd visit him at the station. If he wasn't there when I arrived, he usually showed up before long. He seemed to like me and felt sorry that I had to go trapping with Dad instead of going to school. Dave knew Dad had found a job in a mine. "Maybe you won't have to go trapping anymore now that your dad has found a steady job," he said. "You might be able to go back to school."

I told Dave I thought I was too old to go back to school, but he didn't agree. "It's never too late, nor are you ever too old for anything."

"Mom worries that Dad might just quit his job in the fall and go back to the trapline."

"You know what I would do if I were you and I was tired of trapping year after year?"

"No, I don't."

"Well," he said, "I'd leave home and maybe that's just what you should do. Go somewhere and find yourself a job. You'll be sixteen soon and anybody would hire you. Of course, you might have to go to another province so your dad couldn't get the law after you and bring you home again." He thought for a moment, and added, "There's a lot of nice places in Ontario, just a few miles from the border, where there are gold mines as well as other places to work." He clapped his hand on my back. "If you ever need any help, I'd be more than happy to help you."

When I got home, Mom asked me if I'd had a nice visit with Dave and I told her what we had talked about. "Isn't it funny," she said, "that he should have the same idea I had? And I think it's the only solution. I'm fairly sure that if you weren't here, your dad would be greatly disappointed, but it wouldn't keep him from trapping. However, he probably wouldn't dare go very far into the bush alone any more. He's getting fairly old now and most likely would think twice before attempting to hike more than a few miles away. I could stand that as long as he could come home a few times during the winter."

It was evident that Mom had been mulling over our conversation because it wasn't more than three days later she said to me, "You know, I've been thinking and the more I think about it, the more it makes sense. Paul went to work when he was fifteen and has been working ever since. He seems to be happy; he's saving a bit of money and buying himself a lot of nice clothes. You could do the same; you are no less a man than he was at your age."

"Mom, you can't stay here alone to look after the farm, clear land and do all the chores. That is way too much for a woman. I have to stay and help you while Dad is away working."

But Mom argued that she was able to handle the farm and all the chores. "Who do you think looked after it last winter when you two were away trapping? I did it all alone and I can look after it a lot easier in summer." She insisted, "You go back and talk with Mister Roy again and find out what he had in mind when he said he would be more than happy to help you."

Mom and I talked for almost two hours that afternoon and my head was in a whirl. It was difficult for me to believe she really wanted me to leave the farm, but she was full of encouragement, reminding me of my ability to handle hard work. However, I knew myself better than she did, and I knew I wasn't ready for the outside world. I had barely talked to more than three strangers in my whole life; I had never even been inside a café or a hotel. I didn't know where or how to buy things. I had never been anywhere outside of the trapline or the farm. Then I remembered one of the few conversations Dad and I had had early last fall, shortly after the cabin was built.

We were sitting on the edge of the bed when Dad said, "My friend, your Uncle Albert and I, when we were young, traveled the Ottawa River by canoe from Pembrook all the way to what is Val-d'Or and back to Mattawa, where we spent the winter trapping. I always wanted to go to the head of the Ottawa River just to see where it begins. That's one of the things I promised myself I was going to do when I was twenty, and, by gosh, I am going to see the head of that river before I die."

Dad had carried on that afternoon like I had never heard him before. "The head of the Ottawa River can't be much more than a hundred miles south of our place and we could get there most of the way by water, with maybe just a couple of portages along the way."

That was the longest conversation that had ever taken place between Dad and me in all the time we spent together in the bush. Now, remembering it frightened me. What if Dad decided to trek alone to the head of the Ottawa River next fall? Just thinking of it was enough to keep me from going to sleep that night.

I felt cornered between a rock and a brick wall, but I had to make a decision. I'd just have to go to see Dave and ask him some more questions and prepare myself to leave home. It was better for Mom and me if I left. Dad might be disappointed, but in a way it wasn't the responsibility of either of us to cater to Dad's desires. I hardly slept a wink again that night.

Mom didn't say any more the rest of the week about my leaving the farm. She seemed to have forgotten all about it.

Dad came home that weekend, as he usually did, and he was very grumpy. I couldn't understand why, because everything was going fine on the farm. He left for the mine again early Sunday morning because he had to work the afternoon shift. Shortly after he left, Mom went to work in the garden and a little while later she called me to join her.

Mom was pulling weeds rather erratically, as if she were taking out her frustrations on the weeds. Without looking at me she said, "I don't think your dad will be on that job much longer."

I asked her if Dad had mentioned he wanted to quit.

"Not yet," she replied, "but I know he will soon. I can see the signs already. He's been complaining about having to work shifts and he's not used to doing that. He said he can't sleep during the day and that working in a mine is only fit for someone who can't think for himself, for someone who needs a foreman to tell him what to do and how to do it." I guess Dad carried on for the whole time he was home.

"You go to the house," Mom said, "and change your clothes. Go see Mister Roy and find out if he knows of a place where you can find a job–a place far enough to discourage your dad from going and bringing you home."

Dave seemed happy to see me; at any rate, he greeted me with a big smile. We sat on the bench in the station and I told him Mom had sent me to have a talk with him because she had found out today that Dad was very unhappy in his job and she was afraid he would quit before fall. If so, he would surely go back trapping again and take me with him and that was the last thing she wanted him to do.

Dave asked, "How old are you now?"

I told him I was going to be sixteen on October first.

"Well," he said, "it's only four months away; you won't have any trouble finding a job almost anywhere." Smiling, he added, "Anyone would jump at the chance of hiring a young, strong man like you. I'd even hire you myself, but that wouldn't do you any good because it's too close to home."

We sat in silence for awhile, then Dave said, "One of my brothers-in-law worked in a small town in Ontario and we went to visit him a couple of times. It's a nice, small town where I'm sure you'd feel right at home and it's only a few miles from Rouyn, across the Ontario border. He spent three years working in a mine there and he really liked it, but was forced to quit and move away because of his health."

Dave must have sensed my uncertainty because he said, firmly, "I think that's where you should go–to Kearns. There are two mines there and a fair amount of logging nearby. I'm sure you'd easily find a job and if you didn't, there are other places. Just a few miles farther there's Kirkland Lake where there are several mines, one or two of them located almost in the town itself. I don't see where you'd have any problem at all."

I thanked Dave for his advice and, as I got up to leave, he said, "Whenever you need a hand to get started, just let me know and I'll help any way I can."

When I got home I told Mom what Dave had said and she thought it was a good idea. "Kearns can't be much more than a hundred miles away," she said, "and a hundred miles is not really that far. You and your dad have gone as far as that on snowshoes in the bush. Going to a place like Kearns would be a nice trip by train for you, and a brand new experience. You'd just love it, I'm sure."

As Mom warmed to the subject, she continued, "Tomorrow morning I'm going to leave Roland with the next door neighbor while you and I go to town to get you some new clothes. And I am going to give you fifty dollars; that should be enough for you to get started. Wednesday noon you will flag the train, get on it and buy yourself a ticket to Kearns. Before you know it, you will be off hunting for a job instead of wild animals!"

I lay awake for hours that night, trying to untangle all the ideas crowding my mind. There were so many, I couldn't concentrate on one problem long enough to solve it before my mind was off in another direction.

For instance, it was easy for Mom to say, "Flag the train down, get on it and buy a ticket," but what do I do when I get off the train in a strange town? I suppose I would have to go up to a stranger and ask questions and it wasn't that easy for me to meet strangers, never mind ask them questions. Would they be friendly, or tell me to buzz off?

I thought about Paul, who was having a lot of fun going to movies and pool halls where there were lots of people. But Paul was different from me; he had been talking to strangers since he was ten or eleven. He had gone to town a few times and had played pool before he left home, so he had seen a little of life outside the farm. But I had never been to town yet and I'd be sixteen soon.

The next morning, when Mom told me to get cleaned up and ready to go to town, I shivered a little. However, the idea of her buying me the John Palmer boots I'd seen in the catalogue and had been wanting for so long, soon made my fears disappear and I got ready in a hurry.

Senneterre wasn't nearly as big as I had imagined it to be. There were a few large buildings such as the garage that was on one corner where gas was sold and cars repaired. On the other corner was the theatre and I couldn't resist stopping to take a look at the pictures out front, which were of Jack Benny and somebody named Rochester. The Hudson's Bay store across the street was where Dad sometimes sold our furs. It didn't take us long to make the rounds, including the post office and the railroad station.

We went to Bernard's store and he was standing behind the counter peeling an orange. As Mom explained to Bernard what we were looking for, he tossed the last of the peeling into a wastebasket and popped the whole orange into his mouth. I am sure my eyes got big, as I had never seen anybody eat an entire orange in one bite.

Bernard had the boots I wanted so much and Mom bought them for me, as well as a pair of light brown britches and a jacket to match. When we returned home Mom got busy washing and mending my old clothes, but I was in such a hurry to try my new pants and boots that I put them on and strutted around the house, wishing we had a mirror so I could look at myself.

Alone in my room that night I was once again filled with anxiety. There was a lump in my stomach that just wouldn't go away, even though I had resigned myself to leaving home. After all, if Paul could do it, so could I. And it might be a lot of fun, too, to earn my own money, to be able to go to movies or to pool halls. Mom had warned me that sooner or later I'd have to get out of my cocoon and fly on my own, that I'd have to fend for myself. I knew it had to happen, but I wished I'd had a couple more years before embarking on that journey.

In the morning I did the barn chores as usual, then took a walk around the farm, looking at the work we had done since I'd come home that spring, and at the work that had yet to be done. I knew Mom was going to be very busy and I felt bad that I wasn't going to be there to help her.

The five of us were very quiet at the dinner table that evening. Mom, who had been keeping a sharp eye on the clock, said in a low voice, "It's seven o'clock. You had better get ready to go if you don't want to miss your train. It takes nearly half an hour to walk to the station and you want to get there well ahead of time. Make sure you flag as soon as you see the train coming because it takes a long time for it to stop."

Reluctantly, I picked up my packsack and said goodbye to Noella, Donat and Roland, promising to write each of them. I gave Mom a big hug and kissed her on the cheek. She noticed that I was almost crying and she reassured me that things were going to work out just fine. She made me promise to write as soon as I got settled, even if I didn't have a job yet.

When I got to the road I turned and waved as cheerfully as I could, but my heart was in my throat, threatening to choke me. As soon as I was out of sight I sat down on the shoulder of the road and strongly considered returning home. It was so hard to leave everyone. However, realizing the shame I would face if I did return gave me the strength to go on and I began to walk slowly to the station.

I heard the whistle a few minutes after I got to the station, but I couldn't make myself take the flag and stop the train. In fact, I was almost afraid it might stop to let a passenger off, but it didn't. Leaving home was the hardest thing I had ever done; it almost felt like I was committing the gravest of sins.

It was almost dark and I was still sitting in the station when Dave appeared in the doorway. He had seen my packsack on the platform. "You've missed your train," he said.

"I got here just a bit too late," I lied.

We sat in companionable silence for awhile, then he said, "You don't need to worry; I'll get you on the next freight. I know the brakeman. The freight will take you to Rouyn, maybe not as comfortably as the train, but a lot cheaper. I'm going to make a phone call."

He was back in a few minutes. "There's a freight you can get on that comes by at nine o'clock. Now here's the schedule so you know what's happening: There are four stops between here and Rouyn. The first one is Peron, then Val-d'Or, the next is Malartic, then Cadillac, and the fifth is Rouyn. Keep track of the stops and you can't go wrong."

My head was in a whirl as he continued to explain how to get to my destination. "Rouyn is the end of the C.N. line, but when you get off there you have another forty miles to go. Walk along the railroad tracks for about a mile in the same direction as the freight was traveling and you will come to the T.N.O. station. You can't miss it because the letters are written right on the station. You will have to wait there on the edge of the bushes near the tracks for maybe an hour before you see a freight lined up on a siding. All you have to do is jump in a boxcar, making sure you place a piece of wood in the sliding track of the door so it doesn't slam shut on you, and wait until the freight leaves. The next stop is Chimney and that's where you get off. From there you can get on the road and walk the six miles to Kearns.

I must have looked a little worried because Dave assured me, "You have absolutely nothing to worry about. There are no bulls anywhere along the line yet, so you'd be perfectly safe. There won't be anyone watching for freight jumpers on this line because it's too new and there's not enough traffic on it." Then he cautioned me, "Don't try to jump into a boxcar while the freight is moving; you'll have all the time you need to find an empty boxcar before the train leaves."

One thing puzzled me, so I asked Dave, "What did you mean when you said there were no bulls on this line?"

He laughed. "That's what they call the railroad cops," he said, and at my look of alarm he added, "If I thought you might get into trouble, I wouldn't help you hop a freight. You'll be perfectly safe."

It was totally dark out now and Dave was still coaching me on the new way of life I was about to embark on. "How much money do you have?" he asked.

"Fifty dollars."

"Well, don't keep it all in one wad. Put some in your shirt pocket, some in your hip pocket and keep a small bill in your side pocket so when you need to buy something you don't have to pull out a big wad of bills. And if you rent a room for a night, don't go to one of those flophouses that charges fifty cents a night. Pay a dollar or two and go to a hotel that has rooms with good locks on the doors so you can sleep in comfort and safety."

Dave lighted a match and looked at his pocket watch. "It's a quarter to nine," he said. "The freight should pull in any time now."

I couldn't see his face in the dark, but his voice continued to encourage me. "If there's something you're not sure of, don't leave it to chance. Go up to someone and ask. It doesn't cost anything and you'll be surprised to find that people will be happy to help you."

He was still talking when we heard the freight approaching. We went out to the platform to wait and when Dave saw the brakeman get off to open a switch, he walked over to talk to him. After a few minutes Dave yelled to me to come and bring my packsack. We walked along the train until we came to an open boxcar and David boosted me in, jammed the door with a piece of wood and said, "You're on your way! Good luck to you and don't forget to come and visit us when you get back."

I sat on my packsack in a corner, nervous and uncertain, my legs shaking. The brakeman came by and assured me I was going to be just fine. "Sit down and enjoy the ride," he told me.

The train didn't move for a long time but finally it got going, very slowly at first, but increasing momentum as it went along. It seemed as if it had just reached a good speed when it slowed down again and then stopped. We were in Peron already. Looking out the doorway, I could see the lights of the town in the distance. The next stop was Val-d'Or, a much bigger town, but situated a long way from the station. As I stared at the lights I wondered where Paul was now, and how lucky he was to be able to make his way in such a big city.

When we stopped at Malartic, I saw my first mine. It was very close to town, almost across from the station. The town was well lit and looked like it might be a very pleasant place to live.

Cadillac was a long way from the station; all I could see were a few street lights and some buildings that looked like warehouses. The freight didn't stop there for long.

I had to get off at the next stop, which was Rouyn, the end of the C.N. line, so I placed my packsack near the door and waited. I was just beginning to enjoy the ride and already it was over. When the freight came to a full stop I jumped off and followed the railroad tracks until I saw the large letters on the T.N.O. station. I hid in the willows near the siding and waited.

Rouyn was by far the biggest town I had seen so far. From where I was hiding I could see some men walking up and down the street carrying lunch buckets; even a car would go by now and then.

When I saw a freight lined up on the siding, I found a boxcar and jumped in, once again heading for a corner where I could sit on my packsack and wait. I didn't know what time it was, but I was sure it was getting towards morning. I could see a line of the dawn forming on the horizon and there was already daylight enough to make out the landscape.

After what seemed like a long time the freight began to move and I stood in the doorway to watch the city streets go by. By the time we got to the outskirts of town there was enough daylight to make out the shapes of barns and fences, so I knew we were going through a farming area.

I rested for awhile, but when it was full daylight I stood in the doorway again and now I was watching the forest go by, with huge pine trees and thick green moss covering the ground. It reminded me of the forests closer to home.

The freight came to a stop at a small station, not much bigger than our own flag station. The town was made up of half a dozen houses and I could see smoke rising from a few stovepipes, but there wasn't anyone around the station. I jumped off and looked around; I was still surrounded by a forest of pine trees. There was a narrow road leading the way through the forest. This had to be the road that led to Kearns.

I felt free as I began walking, enjoying the scenery that looked so much like home. Then I realized I was famished so I began to look for a likely spot to stop and eat some of the lunch Mom had packed for me. When I came to a small stream, I got off the road and walked into the bush for a few hundred feet. Standing on the edge of the stream, I got my lunch out and ate a sandwich in much the same manner my dad would have, eating while walking around looking for marten or mink tracks. I spent almost an hour in total relaxation by the creek. It was so peaceful, being all alone, surrounded by the beauty of the forest. Listening to the gentle whisper of the breeze and hearing the birds sing made me almost forget that I had to move on.

After walking about a mile, I came to a highway. Not sure whether to turn left or right, I sat on my packsack for awhile, trying to come to a decision, when I saw a cloud of dust rising in the air. A car went by and soon afterward one more, going in the same direction. I decided to follow the traffic.

I hadn't gone far when a car stopped and the driver yelled, "I'm going as far as Kearns. Can I give you a ride?"

Much too shy and embarrassed to accept, I said, "No, thanks. I'm only going a little ways from here."

Walking slowly along the road I thought: *I have nothing to hurry for. There's lots to eat in my packsack and a whole forest around me that I could call home.* I slowed down even more as I neared town, a bit wary of what was ahead, wanting to put it off for as long as possible. As I crested a small hill I could see Kearns about half a mile ahead so I stopped to gather my thoughts and to decide what to do when I arrived in town.

As it happened, there wasn't time to think for very long. A man came out of the bush no more than a hundred feet from where I was standing. He held a rabbit in each hand. Waving a rabbit at me, he said, "I've had a good catch this morning."

He seemed friendly, so I walked up to him and he greeted me with a warm smile. "My name is Jimmy; what's yours?" he said.

I told him, and he asked, "Coming to visit a relative?"

"No, I've come looking for a job in a gold mine. One of my friends back home had a brother-in-law who worked in one of the mines here and he really liked this town, so my friend suggested I come here."

"What is that brother-in-law's name?"

"Henri Dupuis."

"Oh," said Jimmy, "I knew him. Everybody knows everybody in this town. They were a very nice couple. It's too bad they moved away, but that's how it goes."

Jimmy continued talking as we walked toward town. "It's nice to work underground and make big money, but if a man wants to live to a ripe old age, he shouldn't work there too long. Anyway, you won't have any trouble finding a job here. There's getting to be a serious shortage of men. In fact, with the war taking more and more of them away every day, I wouldn't be surprised to see some of the mines shut down."

When we got to the edge of town Jimmy suggested I try my luck at the mine nearest town. "It's only about a mile to the mine," he said. "In case you can't get in a taxi pool, you can travel that on foot. And if you're looking for room and board right here in town," he pointed to a big brown house, "they say Mrs. Barlow feeds the men pretty good for one dollar a day, and she packs a real good lunch, too. She just might have room for one more."

While I was glad to hear I could probably find a job at the mine, I didn't like the idea of staying in a boarding house with a lot of strangers. That didn't appeal to me at all. I asked Jimmy if there was a place near the mine where I could build myself a cabin, a place in the bush where I could be on my own.

After thinking for a few minutes, he said, "You might not have to build your own cabin. If you want to live alone in the bush, I know a man who has a cabin just a few miles from town. He might rent it to you."

Jimmy told me the man's name was Ed and that he used to be a trapper. "For years he lived alone in that cabin," Jimmy said, "until he got too old and his daughter insisted he move in with them. Now the cabin is sitting there empty."

We walked a bit farther and Jimmy pointed out a small house. "You see the house with the white fence? That's where old Ed lives. If you want, I'll go with you and ask if he'd rent it out."

I said I'd better wait and see if I was going to get a job first, then we'd go and see Ed. Jim went on his way and I carried on through the little town, past the Kearns Arm Hotel and the pool hall. A bit farther I could see a grocery store across the street and a big building over which a sign hung saying Dance Hall. I walked through town, passed a few houses and up a long hill toward the mine. Soon I saw a sign on a high water tank across which was painted Chesterville Mine. There wasn't much to see other than the structure of the shaft house and conveyors and a few men walking back and forth in the yard. I gazed at the scene for a few minutes and walked on.

About a mile past the mine I came to a small stream lined with birch and pine trees. What a welcome and appealing sight! Leaving the road I walked along the stream for some distance, then sat at the base of a big pine tree and watched the fast-running water. It looked so inviting that after awhile I took my clothes off and had a refreshing bath in the ice cold water.

This looked like a good place to camp while I searched for a job, so I packed some rocks, made a fire pit, and broke some boughs for a bed. The food on hand would last until tomorrow when I would go into town and buy groceries.

The next day I bought the food I needed as well as a one-gallon can to steep tea in. I didn't believe in diving into anything too quickly, so I went back to camp to think over the situation and decide what to do next. When I finally made up my mind to go to the mine and ask for a job, I was suddenly in a hurry to get started. I had no idea what time it was, but I had already wasted one day and I wasn't going to put it off any longer. I hung my food high in a tree and started down the highway toward the mine.

When I came to the main gate of the mine I walked in without hesitation. A man was working at a sawhorse and I asked him where they were doing the hiring. He said, "At the office you just walked by, but the captain won't be in until seven o'clock."

"What time is it?"

"It's now six; you have an hour to wait."

I went out and sat on the shoulder of the highway and after awhile two men walked up the road and turned in through the main gate. They sat on the office porch, so I decided to go and wait by the office, too. Standing a few feet away, I could hear their conversation. The younger man, who looked in his early thirties, was telling his friend that he shouldn't even be looking for a job in a mine "Three years working underground is long enough. You should be moving on to some other kind of work."

His friend agreed, saying, "Yeah, if a man wants to live to a ripe old age, three years in a mine is long enough."

"I've been at the same address for too long now," said the younger man. "My wife thinks we should be moving, that it might delay my army call for a few months."

"That's what you should do then, if you think it would delay your call."

They were discussing the same subject when a tall man in his mid-fifties, dressed in khaki pants and shirt, came out of the office. "Come on in, men," he said, and went back into his office.

We filed into the front part of the office where there were a few chairs along one wall. The captain asked the older man to come with him, while we sat down to wait our turn. A few minutes later the man came back, waved a paper at his friend, and went outside to wait for him. The younger man went in next and I could feel fear creeping up on me as I waited my turn, which wasn't long in coming.

"Ever worked in a mine before?" the captain asked me.

Sure that my voice would shake, I decided to keep my answers to a minimum. "No," I answered.

He wrote something on a pad and to my surprise, didn't ask me any more questions. He tore off the piece of paper he had been writing on and said, "You go to the doctor in Virginia Town, whose name is on this slip, and have your medical. When you've got that done, come to the office and we'll sign you up to start work."

CHAPTER VII

When I left the captain's office, I wasn't sure whether I had a job or not and the best way to find out was to ask Jimmy. He would know where Virginia Town was, and how to locate the doctor's office. Why were things so complicated in the outside world?

After almost running the entire one mile to Kearns, I knocked on Jimmy's door and a woman in her mid-sixties answered. She said Jimmy had gone over to his friend Ed's for a few minutes but should be back soon.

"Is there anything I can help you with?" she asked.

"No, I'd just like to ask Jimmy a couple of questions."

"Well, if you want to go and see him, I'll show you where Ed lives."

I thanked her and said I knew where Ed lived, and I headed for the house with the little white fence, half a block from the highway.

Jimmy was sitting on the porch with a much older man whom I presumed was Ed. When Jimmy saw me, he asked in a strong voice that carried for a whole block, "Have you found a job yet?"

"That's what I came to see you about," I said. "I just came from the mine and the captain gave me this slip of paper to go for a medical and I'm not sure if that means I'm hired or not."

Jimmy took the paper, looked at it, and said, "You sure are hired. When the captain sends you for a medical, you can consider yourself hired. Now, I suppose you're looking for a place to live." This was more of a comment that a question.

"Yes, I guess I'll have to find a place now. I'd sure like to rent a cabin somewhere if I could."

"Well," said Jimmy, "I told Ed here that I had met a nice young fella yesterday who hoped to find a job and settle in our town. I said he might be interested in renting a cabin where he could live by himself and he wasn't particular about where the cabin was. I believe Ed will rent his out, isn't that right, Ed?" His voice softened as he turned to the older man sitting beside him. "This is the young fellow I was talking about."

Ed finally spoke for the first time. "Where you from?" he asked.

"Senneterre," I said. "It's in Quebec."

He repeated the name. "Nope," he declared, "the name doesn't mean anything to me. I've been to a lot of places, but I guess I missed that one."

"It's a very small farming town; doesn't make a big dot on the map."

Ed took a stub of a home-rolled cigar out of his shirt pocket, trimmed the soggy end off with his knife, stuffed the rest of it in his pipe and lighted it before he raised his head to look at me.

"My cabin is about a mile from the highway," he said. "I haven't been there for two years now and I suppose you can't even follow the trail anymore–it's probably grown over–but if you can pay in advance, I'll rent it to you for ten dollars a month. That will include the furniture and most of the dishes, but I want you to keep it clean and I will expect the rent paid on time at the end of each month.

I began to search my pockets for the money to pay the rent. There was a five dollar bill in my shirt, but the rest of the money was in my back pocket so there was nothing to do but pull the whole wad out in order to get a ten. While I was busy at that, Ed asked Jimmy what the date was and Jimmy said, "Today is the twelfth of the month."

Ed took a few puffs on his pipe and I could tell he was doing some serious thinking. After awhile he said, "I'll tell you what: you can have the cabin for ten dollars a month and, if you can afford it, you can give me fifteen dollars and your rent will be paid until the end of July."

I handed him a five and a ten and said I would see him at the end of July.

Ed explained that the cabin was located about half way between the two mines. "So," he said, "whichever mine you work at, you'll have a two-mile walk to get to work."

Jimmy told me to see him the next day and he'd show me where the cabin was. "It's well hidden," he said, "among some big pine trees and beside a good-sized creek."

So one problem was solved, but I still had to find out where Virginia Town was. Jimmy said Virginia was about six miles from Kearns and the doctor's office was right on the main drag–I couldn't miss it because his name was written in large letters on the door. I left the two men sitting on the porch and started for Virginia Town, getting there around noon.

There was a card in the window of the doctor's office that said he would be back at one o'clock, so I walked along the sidewalk, looking into store windows. A clock in a restaurant showed twenty after twelve, so I knew I had some time to kill.

Virginia Town was clean, with many red brick buildings, and wide streets lined with big shade trees on both sides. I was very impressed with the town and thought it should be called Virginia City because it was more like a city than a town. I was so busy admiring the town and looking at all the nice things in the store windows that I lost track of the time and when I passed the restaurant clock again I saw it was twenty after one. Even so, after hurrying to the doctor's office, I was hesitant to go in. I had never been to a doctor and was wary about seeing one, but I didn't have much choice. If I wanted to work in a mine I'd have to comply with the rules.

Cautiously opening the door, I was surprised to see just one big room with a desk near the entrance. An older man dressed in a white coat was sitting behind the desk, leaning back in his chair and smoking a cigar.

The man, whom I presumed was the doctor, got up and told me to come on in. He led the way to a corner of the room where he pulled a set of curtains across and told me to shed my clothes. My face must have turned red, I was so embarrassed. When I hesitated, he repeated the order. He stood waiting while I fidgeted with the buttons of my shirt and then, plainly irritated at my slowness, said, "I have an appointment at two o'clock, so let's hurry this up."

Finally I was standing naked in front of him and he looked in my ears, checked a few other parts of me, and took my blood pressure. After the chest x-ray, he told me to get dressed and, as I went past his desk on the way out, he said, "The mine will have my report tomorrow afternoon."

What a relief it was to have that over and done with. Now I could get on with whatever else I had to do in order to start work as soon as possible.

I was hungry as a bear by the time I got back to my camp so I made myself a big lunch. My plans were to go for a walk in the bush until dusk and then go to bed so I could get up early. Instead, I lay down and listened to the sound of the stream, and it was always so easy to go to sleep with that sound in my ears that I fell asleep and had a dream. It began with us kids in the rowboat on our way to pick blueberries. As usual, Dad was at the oars. I was sitting next to Mom, who was fishing, when Dad looked me straight in the eyes and began to sing one of his funny little songs. This one was meant for me:

I know a boy whose name is Gil.
He says he won't, but I know he will
Come trapping with me in the fall

In the bush far, far, away
Where the trees grow big and tall.
He says he won't, but I know he will
Because he knows I need him so.

I woke up, pushed myself against the trunk of a tree and thought about my dream for a long time. It really disturbed me and I debated about what to do: should I go back home, or stay away like Mom wanted me to? After a while I got tired thinking about it and realized it was daylight and I had slept right through the night.

Lighting a small fire near the creek, I steeped a pot of tea and mixed a batch of pancakes. After eating a hurried breakfast, I headed down to meet Jimmy, getting there much too early–there wasn't a sign of life in the house. I hung around the yard for more than an hour before Jimmy saw me through the kitchen window and called for me to come in. He was having breakfast.

"How long have you been waiting in the yard?" he asked.

"Oh, maybe half an hour," I lied. "I always get up too early and I can't sit still."

"Wait until you get older. You'll be slowing down then."

When we got on the road Jimmy said, "I could have met you where you stayed last night. By the way, where have you been staying?":

"By a small stream, just past the first mine. I like it there, it's so much like what I'm used to."

Jimmy chuckled. "That's less than a mile from old Ed's cabin. I bet you're going to like it just fine there, too."

I asked him what Ed used the cabin for and Jimmy said Ed used to be a trapper. "He trapped for most of his life and he stayed in that cabin for months on end. His wife had to go and visit him if she wanted to see him, and sometimes she would spend a week or two there before coming back to town."

I didn't tell Jimmy I had spent five winters in the bush, trapping with my dad. Ed and my dad must be very much alike, I thought, both possessed by the call of the wild, from which they would never be entirely free.

We reached the creek, but instead of turning left off the highway, the way to my camping spot, we turned right. "We should have brought an axe to clear the trail a bit," said Jimmy. "Maybe there will be one at the cabin and we can do some clearing on the way back."

The trail followed the creek most of the way, winding through the pine trees and balsam, with tall poplars on each side of the water. The floor of the forest was covered with thick, rich green moss, and ferns were growing everywhere. There were a lot of grouse in the area, and probably a lot of rabbits, too.

The cabin was a good size: about twenty by eighteen feet, built of peeled logs and chinked with mortar. A huge set of moose antlers hung over the door and a big stack of firewood was piled on either side.

Jimmy retrieved a can from under the porch and produced the key to the front door. The place smelled musty, so we left the door open to air it out. Everything I needed was there: a good stove with an oven, a table and three chairs, and a bed with springs. The mattress was rolled up and hanging from the rafters, as was a roll of blankets. All I had to do was buy some groceries and I could settle in.

We took the mattress and blankets outside to air them out, cleaned the place a bit and then Jimmy showed me the pit a few feet from the creek where Ed kept his bread and vegetables.

On the way back we didn't do anything to the trail; only a few ferns had taken root. It wasn't difficult to walk and the snow-white trilliums would help me stay on the trail after dark.

Jimmy waited for me at the road while I went back to my camp, emptied my packsack and put it on my back. I would need it to cart supplies back from town. When we got to town we parted company and Jimmy made me promise to visit him soon.

I bought groceries, a Big Ben clock, a lunch box and a thermos. I was so used to eating bannock that I didn't think of buying bread to make sandwiches for my lunches.

Walking back to the cabin I noticed a lake a fair distance from the highway and I was glad I had brought my fishing line with me as well as the rabbit snares. I could put both items to good use.

After putting the groceries away I went back to camp and retrieved the rest of my belongings. Once settled comfortably in the cabin, I checked the time on my new clock, which I had set in town. It was only three fifteen, so I had plenty of time to walk to the office and fill out my hiring papers.

The woman at the counter asked if she could help me and I told her my name and said, "The doctor told me his report would be in by this afternoon."

She found the report and handed me some forms to fill out, but when she saw I was having a hard time, she offered to help. With her asking the necessary questions, we were finished in a few minutes. She handed me some more papers and showed me the way to the mine store. Once more I approached a long counter, this time giving my papers to an older man. He asked what size shoes I took. I said, size eight. He leaned over the counter and looked me up and down, assessing my height and waist measurements, and then left the room. When he came back he handed me a belt and hat to try on, showing me how to adjust the lining of the hat. He must have done this often, because everything fit.

He asked me to follow him and we started down a narrow hallway. As we walked, he said, "You should have wool underwear, you know. It's petty cold underground and you have to dress warmly."

We came to the "dry" room, a large area with an adjoining room that contained at least fifty showerheads. There was a sour smell in the room that was hard to describe–a sweaty smell mixed with the odour of soap and burned powder. He showed me my hook where I would hang my dirty mining clothes to dry. Then we walked by the showers and out through a different door.

"Now," he said, "you take these papers to the next building where they're going to tell you when you're supposed to report for work."

Everything seemed so complicated and confused to me that I couldn't figure out how the mine could operate that way. They had a separate building for everything, when one would have been sufficient.

I walked cautiously into the next building and found myself in a long, wide passage with doors on both sides. When I came to a door that was slightly ajar–the nameplate read Jim Baird–I pushed it open slowly. The captain was behind a desk and he recognized me immediately. Seeing the papers in my hand, he stood up and said, "I see you're ready to go to work."

The captain led me to the end of the hallway where there was another long counter with wickets; nameplates were hanging above at regular intervals. The captain stopped at one and said to me, "This is Bob Hearst, your shift boss." He handed Bob my papers, telling him that I had never worked underground before. They chatted for a couple of minutes, then Bob informed me I was on day shift starting tomorrow morning. I should be at the mine around seven o'clock to get dressed, and be at his wicket no later than seven thirty.

The preliminaries were finally over and I got out of that building and away from the smell as quickly as possible. I had never smelled burned powder before, but I was certain that was what caused the horrible acrid odour. What must it smell like in the mine itself, I thought, and if it was that bad, could I adjust to it?

It was with mixed feelings that I returned to my cabin in the woods. Anxious as I was to start on my new job, I was afraid of what new experiences awaited me down in the mine. After making up my bed, lighting the stove and cooking supper, I sat on the edge of the bed and tried to imagine what it might be like underground. How hard would the work be? Would I be able to do it? What if I couldn't, after spending so much money to set myself up? What if I got fired and had to go back home? The questions haunted me for the better part of an hour but in the end I determined that everything was going to work out just fine.

I got my work clothes ready for the next day, but when I started to make my lunch, I realized there was no bread. Hurrying to get done before it got late, I mixed up a batch of bannock and fried it. I had only one shift to work this week, so there would be plenty of time to buy bread over the weekend.

Setting my clock for five thirty, I went to bed, but it wasn't easy getting to sleep with a head full of anxiety about the next day. I consoled myself with the thought that everyone knew I had never worked underground before and they would have to accept my best efforts.

Awake a half an hour before the alarm went off, I got dressed, made breakfast, and was ready long before necessary. I walked slowly to the mine but was still the first one to arrive at the dry room, which wasn't so bad because I had the luxury of putting on my miner's suit without a whole room full of men looking at me.

When the first few men began to file out of the room, I followed them, stopping at Bob's wicket. He handed me a round disk with a number printed on it. "This is going to be your permanent payroll number," he said. "You follow the men to the shaft house and wait for me there. I'll be along soon and assign you a partner."

In the shaft house I sat on a dynamite box as most of the men did, and waited apart from everyone else so I could take in all there was to see. The cage had been going up and down for a long time, carrying men to the bottom, when my shifter showed up. He was a tall, husky, dark man of about forty. Bob pointed me out to him, told him my name, and said, "This is your new partner." Then he said to me, "This is John. You do whatever he tells you to do and the two of you will get along just fine." John stood waiting near the cage door. Neither of us said a word.

When the cage came again, we got in and started down, only to stop a couple of minutes later. John got off first and we headed up a drift. "We are on level four here," he said, "If you ever become disoriented, find your way here, sit down and don't move Someone will come along and you can ask them to guide you back to the job." As we walked up the drift we were totally dependent on our battery lights, which I thought was neat.

We climbed some ladders, came to a sort of tunnel and John explained that we were in sub-drift number four. Making a right turn we continued to walk a few hundred feet farther when we came to a large room cut out of solid rock. There was equipment lying in a pile of muck and dust and the walls were covered thickly with the same kind of muck. It smelled the same as the dry room only much stronger.

John sat down on a piece of planking and opened his lunch box. After eating a sandwich, he lighted a cigarette and drank a cup of coffee. All the while, I sat on an empty dynamite box, waiting for him to tell me what to do. Nearly a half hour passed and I was beginning to feel cold when he finally got up, grabbed a piece of gear and began to set up a machine that I later realized was a drill. When he was ready, I helped him lift the liner on the cross arm and raise it to the top of the bar. He showed me where to turn the air on and said I'd have to do that every day thereafter when he was ready to start.

We came back to the machine and John began drilling. The noise was ear-splitting. I retreated to the entrance of the sub-drift to get away from the noise a bit, and when I looked back all I could see was a cloud of dust completely engulfing John. I found a spot to sit down and after awhile my ears much have become accustomed to the noise because it didn't seem so bad any more.

After drilling for a couple of hours, John stopped the machine and came up to me. "There should be a set of drilling steels at the station by now," he said. "Go down there and bring them here. You'll find a lorry nearby that you can load them onto."

It felt strange, walking alone in such deep darkness, and I had to wait at the station until the cage tender arrived with the set of steels. After loading the lorry, I pushed it up to the sub-drift and brought seven or eight steels to John, who was sitting down eating his lunch by then. It was unbelievable how fast the first part of the shift had gone by.

John went back to work, but before long he had orders for me. "Go back to the station and wait there for the cage tender to deliver the dynamite," he said, "and bring it up as soon as it gets there."

Shortly after I got to the station the dynamite came, along with a big coil of fuses and a box of caps. The lorry was soon loaded and John had the supplies he was waiting for. I watched as he loaded the round, fascinated with the deftness with which he inserted the dynamite in the holes, with the fuses hanging neatly, then gently tamped the dynamite with a long wooden dowel.

Before he was finished loading John told me to go to the station and stay there, which I did. It wasn't long before John and the other miners arrived and we waited together for the cage to take us up.

While we were waiting, John asked me, "How do you like your job so far?"

I told him it was just fine, but I was disappointed that I didn't have much work to do.

"You should be happy you're not overworked," he replied. "Just wait and see, the hard work will come as you get more experienced. Never complain because you don't have enough work to do." The other men nodded in agreement.

The worst part of the day for me came at the end of the shift when we all got to the dry room. Every man got undressed and walked stark naked to the shower room. It was so embarrassing to stand there nude where everyone could see me, but no one seemed to look at anyone else. They washed themselves while talking in a normal way about their day's work and, as time went by, I got over my embarrassment and didn't feel so uneasy.

Back at the cabin I was very happy to have put in one shift. It would have been nice to know how much money I had earned that day, but I hadn't asked what the wages were. Jimmy would probably know and I had to go to town for bread the next day, so I would stop at his place and ask him.

I got to town just as the store was opening and I bought two loaves of bread. Afterwards I went to see Jimmy and told him how the job went. He was happy that I had gotten along all right and when I asked him about the wages, he said, "Starting wage at the mine is sixty-three cents an hour."

He seemed sure about his facts, but I couldn't believe it. "Whoa, Jimmy! That's a lot of money," I protested.

"Just ask your machine man; he'll tell you. If you're helping on a drill, you might get a bit of a bonus, too."

On my way home I stopped by the pool hall and looked through the window. It looked very inviting, but I wasn't going to play a game until I got my first paycheck, whenever that was. At any rate, I didn't plan to stay in town long because I had my fishing line with me and I wanted to see if I could catch myself a fish for dinner.

Without bothering to look for a trail to the lake, I just zigzagged my way through the bush for about a half a mile until I came to a spot where the water looked fairly deep, and I baited my hook. The lake wasn't nearly as nice as most of the lakes I had seen and I doubted whether I would have any luck, but I got a strike right away, and then another. I was happy to go home with two northern pike.

The rest of the day was spent washing clothes and writing a letter to my mother, who I was sure was waiting to hear from me. It was a long weekend as I didn't have to go back to work until midnight Monday–the graveyard shift that every miner detested.

Over the next three weeks there was no time to get lonesome. I didn't sit around the cabin long enough to have time to think about home, but always found something to keep myself occupied. There was firewood to cut, rabbit snares to set and, of course, making the rounds of my snares was another excuse to get out of the cabin. Once a week I'd bake a big pot of pork and beans and mix a batch of bannock, so time went by rapidly.

On the tenth of July I got my first paycheque, which wasn't very big. Two weeks had been held back, and after my miner's clothes had been deducted there was just over three dollars left. John told me the grocery store would cash my cheque if I bought groceries there. I had plenty of food except for bread, so I bought two loaves and got the balance of my check in cash.

Having promised myself a game of pool when I got paid, I headed for the pool hall but was surprised to find the place empty. The older man behind the counter said, "If you're looking for a partner, you'll have to find one at the hotel. That's where everybody goes on payday." Not wanting to hunt for a partner, I went back to the cabin.

The next day I hung around town a bit to learn what went on in a mining town. When I came to the pool hall again I decided to go in and buy myself a bottle of pop, which I had never tasted before. Paul had told me how delicious it was, and I was curious.

While I was drinking my pop a man in his late forties walked in–a big, husky man at least six foot tall and over two hundred pounds. He had a receding, reddish hairline, a very friendly smile and big blue eyes. He bought a package of tobacco and exchanged a few words with the man behind the counter, then came over to me and asked if I wanted to play a game of eight ball. I told him I had never played pool and he said, "It's easy. I'll teach you how. Grab a cue."

"How much does it cost?" I asked.

"Don't worry about it. I'll pay for the games."

When I heard that, I hurriedly grabbed a cue before he could change his mind. He asked me my name, and told me his was Joe. "I have a boy looks to be about your age," he said. "How old are you?"

We played four games and Joe won them all. When we said goodbye we made plans to meet there again next weekend. Mom had told me I would meet some very nice people when I was on my own, and she was right.

My job at the mine was going well and I liked it more and more every day. John had gradually become more friendly and he'd sit and talk with me about mining and about his family. He said I was the best helper he'd ever had and that his bonus had taken a big jump since I began working with him. That made me feel good.

Not long after I began work I had noticed John picking up rocks here and there and putting them in a small white cotton bag. When I asked what he was doing, he said he was picking up samples for the shifter.

"That's what determines my bonus–how rich the stope is in gold," he explained, "and the more samples I pick up, the bigger my bonus is."

To help John get a bigger bonus I asked him to show me what type of rock he needed, and after that I'd spend the better part of my day picking up samples. It was fun and gave me something more to do. John would go up at the end of the shift with a bag full of samples, but I wasn't supposed to tell anyone because some of the other miners might come and get samples from his stope and he didn't want that to happen.

Next Saturday morning I went to town again, taking along my fishing line and a pocket full of bait. I needed to buy bread and wanted to do a bit of fishing on my way back to the cabin. Joe was sitting on a bench in front of the pool hall when I came out of the store, so I sat down beside him.

I asked Joe which of the mines he used to work at and he said, "Both of them, but I had to give up the mines a couple of years ago. My health gave out and now I'm working in a logging camp a few miles from town."

"Did you like working at the Chesterville?" I asked.

"Oh, yes, it was great working there but the bonus wasn't very good so I quit and went to work at the Kerr Addison Mine, a couple of miles farther down the highway. I worked there for over a year and that's when my health took a turn for the worst." He sighed and continued, "I sure wish I could go back. I'd make a lot better money working underground than in a logging camp and I need to earn big money to support my large family."

Joe said he had nine children and the oldest boy was seventeen. "He's beginning to find the odd job here and there," he said, "and he gives all his money to his mother, but I don't know how things are going to turn out for us. My health is getting worse all the time. Now I have a bleeding ulcer so I have to be careful of what I eat. I keep getting these horrible heartburns; it's getting so bad I can't even sleep at night."

When Joe had finished telling me his troubles, he said he'd like to play a few games of eight ball with me, but he didn't have any money. "I sent my check to my wife and didn't even keep enough to buy myself tobacco for the next two weeks."

Hearing Joe's story had made me feel really bad for him, so I said, "Let's go in and I'll pay for the games this time. It's my turn."

We played one game and then Joe borrowed a dime so he could buy a pack of tobacco. When he got back to the table, he realized he didn't have any cigarette paper, either, so I gave him another nickel. We played three more games and I won two of them, which made me feel pretty good.

The next time I saw Joe was payday at the end of the month and I was in town to cash my check and buy groceries. Joe was coming in just as I walked out of the store. He seemed happy to se me.

"I didn't come down last weekend," he said. "We had to work all the way through. They were getting ready to shut the camp down because the forest is too dry and they're afraid of a forest fire. We only finished work yesterday afternoon." He shook his head sadly. "I slept in the bushes behind the hotel last night, had to send my wife my whole paycheck again and was left flat broke. Do you think you could lend me five dollars until I get back to work? I promise I'll repay you out of the first check I get."

Of course I loaned Joe the five although, after spending nearly twelve dollars for food it didn't leave me much out of my forty-eight dollar check. In fact, I didn't have as much money as I had when I left home!

We crossed the street and sat on the bench in front of the pool hall, but I didn't suggest we go in and play a game. We just sat in silence for awhile and then Joe asked me if I was still picking up samples for my machine man.

"Yes," I said. "Every day John has a full bag of samples to take up with him. He's sure happy to have me as a partner."

Joe shook his head. "You know, you should get smart. Have you ever seen John give that bag of samples to your shifter, or the captain, or even leave it somewhere for them to pick up? No!" he said. "I'm sure you didn't see John do that because he keeps it for himself. He's high-grading–that's what we call it. John is getting you to help him steal gold from the mine."

At my shocked expression, Joe advised "Get wise and keep it for yourself. You can walk out of the mine with at least six or seven dollars worth of gold every day, and that's a lot more than you make in wages. I worked there and I know, almost everybody is high-grading. Nobody checks to see if you're taking anything out. If you do get some gold out of there, I'll help you sell it and we'll both wind up making money."

I quickly told Joe that I was making good enough wages and had plenty to live on. I wasn't about to start stealing gold from the mine. But he cut in before I was finished talking. "You call sixty cents an hour good money when the mine-owners are getting one million dollars a month out of the gold in that mine? They're so rich they don't know what to do with their money. You better take a good, long look at the situation; you'll realize they are taking advantage of the miners."

It was dark when I got up to go back to my cabin. "Thanks for the five," Joe said, "I'll see you next weekend, I hope." I told him I'd be in town and would see him then.

What Joe had told me certainly set me to thinking. I was going to keep a sharp eye on John for the next week or two and see what he did with the sample bag at the end of the shift.

When John told me to head for the station just before lighting the fuses, I walked around the corner, turned my light off and waited. A few minutes later I saw John place the sample bag in his lunch box and close the lid. When he began to light the fuses I ran to the ladders and all the way to the station so that I was sitting there waiting when John came in. I was the first one out of the shower room, so I went over and picked up John's lunch box. It was much heavier than it should have been.

While I slowly got dressed, I kept an eye on John, pacing myself so I was ready when he was. He picked up his lunch box, walked out of the door just ahead of me and down the road toward home.

On the way home that night I did a lot of thinking. Obviously, Joe knew what he was talking about.

On the job the next day I never let it show that I knew what was going on. I kept picking up samples for John as usual until I found a big, beautiful chunk of rock. There was so much gold in it all I could see was a narrow line of blue quartz running through the centre–almost a pure nugget!

If John could do it, so could I. I decided at that moment that this nugget was mine. Later I placed it in the brown paper bag I kept my lunch in, rolled it up, stuffed it into my lunch box and closed the lid. But when I came out of the cage and into the dry room I felt so guilty I was sure everyone was staring at me as if they all knew I had a piece of high grade in my lunch box. Suddenly, I was very sorry I had decided to take that beautiful rock.

When I got safely back to my cabin after work I heaved a huge sigh of relief. Taking out the nugget, I looked at it for a long time before placing it on a window sill by the table where I could admire it. As I sat looking at it, I thought: So Joe was right; my partner is getting me to help him steal gold. It wasn't something to be proud of, and I heartily wished I had never discussed it with Joe.

On Saturday I went to town to buy groceries, get my mail and maybe visit with Jimmy for a few minutes. I didn't take my fishing line with me this time because I couldn't stay away too long. I had clothes to wash and bannock to make, and I had to put some beans to soak to get them ready for the next day. There was plenty to do, and I wasn't going to waste much time I town.

Just as I arrived at the store and began to pick out a few supplies, Joe came in. He looked terrible: his face was drawn and pale, and he walked like an old man of seventy. I asked what was wrong.

"Oh," he said, "it seems that everything is wrong. I've been sleeping out in the bush for the whole week and my rheumatism is killing me. I can't live this kind of life, sleeping on the ground and eating one meal every second day. It's getting so bad that sometimes I feel like throwing myself in the lake and putting an end to my misery. And now I'm even losing courage, because I know I can't earn enough money to ever get out of the hole and support my family properly. It seems like I have nothing left to live for."

My soft young heart melted like butter in a hot frying pan and my big mouth just opened up. "You can come and live with me until the camp reopens," I said. "You'll have to sleep on the floor, but at least you'll be warm and dry and it's a lot better than sleeping out in the bush. And you can eat three good meals a day, too. It will be company for me–someone to talk with when I'm at home. How about it, Joe?" I asked.

"It's very generous of you to do that for me, and maybe I'll take you up on it, but you can be sure I'm going to repay you for everything you do for me. It's just that now I'm in a black hole and can't seem to get out of it."

We walked back to the cabin together, and I was glad to have someone to help me carry the one hundred pounds of flour I had just bought. While I put the groceries away, Joe walked around looking at everything and of course he spotted the nugget I had placed on the windowsill.

"Ha, ha, I see you have been doing a bit of high-grading," he exclaimed, picking up the nugget and examining it.

"I only took that one piece because it was so perfect I just couldn't resist."

After looking at the nugget carefully, Joe said, "You have about thirty to forty dollars worth of gold here—the equivalent of two weeks' wages. You see, if you did that twice a week, you would make a hundred dollars extra a month. And with me as a partner, since I know all about the black market, I could sell it for you at a small percentage and we would both be making good money. That's just what I need right now, to make some big money to enable me to catch up on my bills and get back on my feet."

I listened to Joe, taking in everything he said, but not saying a word myself. The groceries put away, I told him I had to make the rounds of my rabbit snares and would be back in half an hour.

After following the narrow trail for awhile I sat down at the base of a tree to do some heavy thinking. Was it worth the risk, to help Joe get back on his feet? The tussle with my conscience went on for a long time and in the end I came to no decision one way or the other; my mind was too muddled to make a clear assessment of the situation.

When I came back to the cabin Joe was at the stove, making a pot of pea soup. "If I'm going to be eating here," he said, "I guess I can do some of the cooking. I'm a fairly good cook and my specialty is pea soup; it doesn't bother my ulcer."

Picking up the nugget, I went over and sat on the bed. Joe turned around and saw me. "You know," he said, "when I worked at the Kerr Addison Mine, I drilled one of the stopes on the fourth level where the high grade was so pure you could cut it out of the walls with a pocket knife. If ever you want to see free gold, that's the mine to work in. A man could get very rich in a few weeks if he was smart enough to figure out a way of getting the gold off the mine property, and I think I have figured out the only way it can be safely done."

Sensing my interest, he continued, "I bet I'm the only man who has ever studied the possibilities of getting gold out of the Kerr Addison, and I bet I could get gold out of there by the ton; easy as stealing candy from a baby."

By now I was clinging to every word he said, but still skeptical. "So, how come it would be so easy?" I asked.

He smiled, obviously glad I had asked the question. "That was the reason I went to work there–to steal gold–and not just a few nuggets, either. But then I found out how tight the security was. Security is so tight, no one can get past the shaft house with gold. As you come out of the cage, you have to place your lunch can on a belt and a security man checks every part of it, even to dismantling your thermos. Then you shed your mining clothes and go for a shower. When you come out, you walk naked past the metal detectors on your way to a set of stairs that takes you to another dry room where you put on your street clothes."

Joe put down the soup ladle and sat at the table. "I knew I'd never be able to get any gold out that way, so I began to study the surface. I just knew there had to be a loophole somewhere." His eyes glistened as he continued. "The property is surrounded by a twelve-foot fence, and the top wire carries a twelve-thousand-volt current. I spent many evenings scanning the ground with a set of binoculars and noticed there were four manholes and one of them went all the way down to the sixth level. Each manhole is covered with a small shed, equipped with a punch clock. There's a guard who comes around every hour to punch the clock and then go on to the next one."

Joe was getting more and more excited as he told me about his plan. He elaborated on every phase, as excited as if we were going to pull the job the next day.

"There is a big pine tree just inside the fence," he said as he scribbled, drawing diagrams on a piece of my writing pad he had pulled down from the shelf. "Below it is a big, high boulder that rises almost to the top of the fence. With a piece of plank and a rope, we could crawl along one of the branches, past the top wire of the fence, and jump down on the boulder. Presto! We're inside the mine property, and from there it is easy sailing. But someone has to work at the mine to stash the free gold at a certain spot, then all we have to do is get down and retrieve it. Simple as that."

It seemed a bit too easy to me, but we sat for a long time, looking at his plan. Finally he said, "The more I look at this, the more I'm sure the two of us could get very rich in two or three weeks. You could quit your job tomorrow and get another one at the Kerr Addison the very same day. You'd be earning the same money and probably doing the same type of work, and after a few weeks you would never have to work again. Doesn't that sound good?" He was silent then, looking at me for an answer.

"Joe," I said, "you make it sound easy, but I'm not convinced that there aren't any big risks involved. What would happen if we were caught? We'd both go to jail for a long time."

Joe took a deep breath. "I'll tell you what, You get yourself a job there and stash as much gold as you can. When you have about one hundred pounds of it ready, you carry on working and I'll go down alone and retrieve the gold and we'll split the money. That way, you're not getting involved in stealing anything. They can't do a thing to you if they catch you stashing gold on their property. Your hands will be clean. I'll take the risk of getting the gold out of the mine, but I don't mind doing it alone. What do you say to that?"

Once again I told Joe I wasn't prepared to make a decision right away. I wanted to think about it and would let him know later.

Joe made his bed on the floor and he snored all night, but was up early enough to have breakfast ready when I got up. He was in a good mood, saying it was the best night's sleep he'd had in a long time.

I went to work and it was the worst day I ever had on the job. I ran myself ragged to no avail. John was cranky; everything went wrong and he blamed me for it all.

In the dry room the next morning I was talking to the man next to me and I told him how cranky John had been the day before. "He gave me a really bad time," I said.

"I don't doubt that a bit," he said. "I live next door to him and I know him well. He'd been drinking all weekend and fought with his wife, who drinks as much as he does. That's one of the reasons he has so much trouble keeping a steady partner. He blows up and even threatens to kill his helper. A few months ago he hit his partner across the head with a six-foot steel, busted his hard hat. The guy took the cage up and quit the same day."

After hearing that I wasn't too anxious to go back down in the mine, but I told myself I had picked enough samples for him; he wouldn't do that to me.

Things were going fine; John was drilling his last hole when a steel jammed and he couldn't pull it out. I went over to help and without any warning he gave me a vicious shove that sent me flying onto a pile of muck, nearly breaking my ribs. He was in such a total rage, cursing and swearing at me, that I got scared and ran out of the stope and down to the station to safety. After sitting on a bench for nearly an hour the first miner showed up and soon they were all in except John, who missed the cage that night. I was so scared I didn't care what happened to him.

When I got back to the cabin I told Joe what John had done, how scared I had been, and asked him what I should do about it.

Joe said, "You can't take a chance with a man like that. Your best bet is to quit and work somewhere else. You never know, the man could go stark, raving mad and kill you, especially if he suspected you knew about him stealing gold. If he thought you would turn him in, it would be easy for him to kill you and make it look like an accident."

"So, what are you saying?"

"If I were you, I'd go to your shifter in the morning and tell him you quit. If he asks why, you just tell him you don't like working underground and that you found another job you like better. Don't tell him it has anything to do with your machine man. If John ever found out you said anything about him—something that could get him fired—he might come after you."

I guess Joe could see my uncertainty because he said, "I'm sure the shifter will understand and won't make a fuss about you quitting. He'll just tell you to pick up your check when it's ready. You'll only lose one day's work if you go to the Kerr Addison at four o'clock tomorrow afternoon. You'll get hired, go for your medical the next day, and start work the day after that. Nothing to it."

It was almost as hard for me to quit my job as it was to apply for it, but I did it.

CHAPTER VIII

I went to my shifter's office early the next morning and told him I was quitting. "I don't want to work in the mines any more," was all the explanation I gave.

He didn't question my decision, just asked for my badge and crossed my name from his manifest. My check would be ready that afternoon. Relieved, I went out of the door for the last time, without having to face any of the men I had worked with.

When I returned to the cabin I felt kind of sad and needed some time alone, so I told Joe I was going for a walk in the bush. It was so nice to be alone in the forest where there was no pressure on me, where I could sit down anywhere I pleased and think without interruption. It was much easier to sort things out in solitude and I had a lot of sorting to do in order to put my life back on track.

Taking out the three letters Mom had sent me in the time I had been away, I sat on the green moss at the foot of a big pine tree, and reread them. In the first, she said how happy she was that I had found a job, as she had been sure I would. Things were fine at home, etc. She ended by saying, "Don't work any harder than you have to, and don't forget to say your prayers."

The second letter was much the same, except that she mentioned Dad a little more. He wasn't very happy with his work. He felt like slave—having to start at the whistle and quit at the whistle—and that wasn't what freedom was about, he said. But he had not yet mentioned quitting.

The last letter had come just a few days ago, and in that one she talked about Paul and Gemma. She saw more of Gemma now because she had a boyfriend and they came together to visit on weekends. Mom was happy for her. She said Paul had been charmed by a fast-talking salesman into investing money in some scheme, and had lost it, but was still working at Val-d'Or. She warned me to be careful of wolves disguised as sheep, that there were many of them and they all had tempting offers but they would take everything you've got, even your body and soul. Be careful of who you trust, she ended, and don't forget to say your prayers.

It was long past noon when I got back and Joe wasn't at the cabin, but he had left a pot of rabbit stew simmering on the stove. The smell of it reminded me of how hungry I was. It was the best rabbit stew I had ever tasted, with lots of big chucks that had the tangy taste of wild meat, and a thick brown gravy to sop my bannock in. I had to admit it; Joe was a lot better cook that I was.

It was about a quarter after three when I began walking to the mine. After waiting at the gate for some time, another man showed up and I asked if he was a miner. "Not yet," he said. "I've never worked in a mine before."

When we got called in, I was the first to be interviewed. The captain asked if I had worked in the mines before and I told him I had worked as a driller's helper at the Chesterville Mine. "Well," he said, "you'll start at the bottom here." He filled out a slip for me to give to the doctor and told me to come back in a couple of days.

I was home when Joe returned just before dark and I could detect a funny smell on his breath. When I asked him what he'd been eating, he said, "I haven't had a bite to eat since I left here, but I met one of the crew I was working with and he bought me a few beers. We sat in the pub the best part of the afternoon, talking about the job." Joe looked pretty downcast as he continued. "It looks like they're not going to reopen the camp, which means I'm out of a job and I don't know what I'm going to do."

I felt bad for Joe, but there wasn't much I could do to help. I told him I had been hired by the mine and was going for my medical in the morning. He seemed happy for me.

Nervous about the new job, I tossed and turned all night. Meeting new people was hard for me and I wondered how everything would turn out. There was so much going on all the time, I wondered if it was worth the struggle trying to keep up with civilization. Life was so much simpler in the bush where you could come and go at your own convenience, with no one around to hurry you. I could see why Dad liked the wilderness so much.

Early the next morning I started out toward Virginia Town, getting there long before the doctor's office opened. Once again I walked about the streets, looking in store windows, but I felt more at ease this time. Even getting undressed for the doctor's exam didn't faze me, and I had nerve enough to ask him if he could hurry his report because I wanted to start work as soon as possible. He told me if I waited a few minutes, he would finish it and I could take it with me.

The office at Kerr Addison was much bigger than the one at Chesterville, and a lot brighter. It was like two different worlds. The office was staffed with younger women who dressed better and were much more friendly. I handed my doctor's report to an attractive young blond clerk who read it, dropped it into a wire basket, and proceeded to fill out a set of hiring forms for me. When that was done she nodded toward the captain's office and said, "This way, please."

I told the captain, Jed Parr, that I had my miner's suit and the rest of my gear, so he took me out and introduced me to my shifter, Ernie Leblanc. Ernie must have needed help because he asked me right away if I could start work that afternoon on the four o'clock shift. I assured him I could.

I hurried back to tell Joe about my good fortune—that I wasn't going to miss even one day's work but would start that very afternoon. Joe looked pretty downcast, so while I was making lunch I asked if there was anything wrong.

"Well," he said, "I feel like a bum, sponging off you like this."

When I tried to interrupt, he waved me off. "Don't get me wrong. I appreciate everything you're doing for me, it's just that I hate being in the position I'm in and wish I could do something about changing it. But one day I'll repay you for everything." After getting that off his mind, Joe asked me what my job was going to be.

"I don't know exactly, Joe," I answered. "The shifter hasn't told me yet."

Before I left for work I asked Joe to wish me luck. "I'll tell you all about my first day when I get back in the morning."

The office at Kerr Addison was not the only part of the mine that was different from Chesterville. To my surprise, the dry room was also an improvement. There wasn't that sour acrid smell and the walls had been freshly painted.

After putting on my miner's suit, I headed for the shifter's wicket where Ernie issued me a metal badge and told me to wait for him in the shaft house.

Sitting on an empty dynamite box, I waited anxiously for Ernie. Meanwhile, I sized the place up, counting the men as they came in. There seemed to be about the same number of men working there as at Chesterville, so I figured the mines were about the same size.

Ernie finally arrived, accompanied by a young man about my age, maybe a year older, whom he introduced as Raymond. "You two are going to be working together," Ernie said. "Raymond here knows what there is to be done. All you have to do is follow him and make sure you don't get lost. Your job is to clean up. You pick up all the garbage, broken steels and empty dynamite boxes, starting at the first level and on to the last one. You shouldn't have any trouble; Raymond here has been doing it for some time now and knows every corner of the mine."

After Ernie was gone Raymond explained that we would ride the last cage down to the first level and work our way down from there.

He seemed to be a nice guy. He, too, was from a farm but he had a lot more trouble with English than I did. In fact, he had a hard time making himself understood. I was lucky that my dad had taken the time to teach his kids a bit of English, explaining that we lived in a bilingual country and if we wanted to see the world, we should speak both languages.

The cage came and we went down to the first level. The station was well lit and the walls were painted white. So far it seemed to be a lot drier than the Chesterville Mine.

We did like all miners do, we sat at the station and poured ourselves a cup of tea or coffee, as the choice might be, then Raymond began explaining to me what our duties would be. First of all, he said, we don't have to report to the shift boss; in fact, we would seldom see him.

After what might have been about one-half hour, Raymond grabbed his lunch can and told me to do the same, saying we'd have to carry it with us through the shift as we didn't know where we might be at lunch time.

I took my lunch can and followed him as he started to walk along a drift. We'd walked for a couple of hundred feet when we came to a raise and climbed two sets of ladders about twenty feet each. It was very wet in the raise, with water dripping heavily on us. We found ourselves in a large room cut out of solid rock. We left our lunch cans near the raise that was equipped with a tugger hoist. Raymond explained again that we were going to go around the stope and bring back all the debris we found here, then we'd load it all in the skip and lower it to the level below.

I said to Raymond, "The job is easy and very simple. We don't really need a boss." He agreed with me, saying that he liked the job just fine, if it wasn't for having to have to go down the ladders where it was so wet, with ice cold water running down our sleeves.

When I got back to the cabin shortly after one o'clock, Joe was still up waiting for me. He asked me how my shift went and I told him I liked the job. "It was a lot more fun than helping on a drill. All we have to do is go around the whole mine picking up garbage and debris left behind by the miners."

Joe grinned at me and said, "Why, you're a nipper–that's what they call your job. That's good; you couldn't have landed a better opportunity to high-grade. You go to all the richest stopes in the mine and end your shift on the very last level where there's a crosscut I know of where they used to store mine timbers. It's a perfect place to hide high grade. What you have to do now is try to be left alone in one of the rich stopes long enough for you to pick up a few pounds of high grade and hide it. I'm sure you could hide eight or ten pounds of it every day."

The more Joe talked, the more excited he became. "I'm going to draw you a diagram of the sixth level so you know where the crosscut is that I mentioned. You'll see how nicely it fits into my plan, and it's as safe to hide high grade there as it would be to deposit it in a bank. We couldn't have it any better than this."

He couldn't wait to outline the plan. "You work a few shifts to get well acquainted with the surroundings, all the while looking for a crosscut that's only a few feet past the john. Everybody has to go to the bathroom," he explained. "You see if they still store timber in it, and if they do, that's the best place to hide high grade. Hardly anyone ever goes there and it's not far from one of the rises that goes to the surface."

Joe sat down and began to draw a diagram of the mine, and from the little I had seen it looked very accurate. He pin-pointed all the small details. "You start here," he said, making a pen mark on the diagram, "and you go down to the second level, and so forth. Here on the fourth level,"and he circled the area, "is the richest stope in the mine. It's the second stope on your right." He traced a line to the far wall of his chart. "You can cut nuggets off the wall with a pocket knife, and you'll see all kinds of it lying among the rocks on the floor as well. From there you only have two levels left to go before the end of your shift. You won't have any trouble picking up ten pounds of high grade, stuffing it in your bag and taking it down to the sixth level. When you get there, tell your partner you have to go to the john while he goes to the station. You hide the high grade, go back to the station and in just a few shifts you'll have well over a hundred pounds of high grade worth thousands of dollars.

We were up until daylight, with Joe talking and making plans. Finally, I told Joe I was tired and had to go to bed because I wanted to go to the office to get my cheque the next day.

Joe was already outside cutting firewood when I woke up just after ten o'clock the next morning. He came in when he heard me cooking breakfast. "You know," he said, "I'm nearly fifty now and I've been around a lot in my life, and among all the people I've known, you are the best friend I've ever had. Nobody has ever done so much for me and I'm sure grateful. I just don't know what I'd have done if I hadn't met you." He stood on one foot and then the other, as if embarrassed.

"I can honestly say you saved my life, because I was very close to ending it by jumping off a bridge. It's really something for me, to think I have a friend like you." With that, he turned and went back outside before I could think of anything to say.

I was not used to such praise and I must admit it boosted my ego.

After breakfast, I picked up my cheque from the mine and went to town. I cashed the check and bought a couple of loaves of bread and a pack of Zig Zag tobacco for Joe. When I got back Joe was finishing his dinner. I gave him the tobacco and told him I was going to lie down until it was time to get ready for work. He seemed really pleased about the tobacco, but didn't say much.

At the mine Raymond and I went down together as usual, but when we came to the fourth level and into the stope Joe has said was so rich, I told Raymond we should split up. If he took one side and I took the other, I explained, we'd finish a lot sooner and we could meet at the rise.

Raymond agreed, so I took the right side and he the left. I had a good chance to look for high grade, and saw lots of it, but I didn't take any that day, even though I was very tempted.

We met at the rise, which was equipped with a tugger hoist and a small bucket used to send the refuse down to the lower level. It wasn't difficult to operate: you just pulled the lever to make it go down and pushed it to make it go up. It was Raymond's job to run the hoist, but that day he agreed to let me try. The bucket landed smoothly at the bottom and Raymond was impressed. "You did a better job than I do," he said. "I think you can do it all the time from now on."

At the end of the shift we walked down the ladders, with Raymond again complaining about getting wet from head to foot. He was still complaining when we got to the last station, so I told him, "You know, if you hate walking down the ladders so much, I can let you down in the bucket. I don't mind so much getting wet myself." He said he'd think about it.

Joe was still up when I got home and it was evident that he wanted to talk to me. I'd only been home a short time when he said, "My friend...." He sounded exactly like my dad did when he wanted me to do something he thought I might refuse to do. "My friend, I haven't seen my wife and family for over two months now and I really miss them. If you were kind enough to lend me five dollars, I'd go home tomorrow for a short visit."

If Joe had not used the same opening my dad did, I don't think I would have loaned him the money, but now all I could think of was it would be like turning my dad down if he asked me for a loan, and I couldn't do that. I went outside where my money was buried, pulled the can out of the hole, took five dollars out and gave it to Joe.

When I got up just before noon, I was alone, but Joe had left a note for me. He said how much he appreciated my lending him the money. He was sorry he had to leave so early and didn't have a chance to say goodbye, and that he should be back in three or four days. It felt good to be alone in the cabin again and to be able to go freely about the place without having to try to please someone else.

After awhile I realized it was Saturday and I didn't have to go to work that night I went outside and got my money and counted it. I had more than two hundred dollars, and my rent was already overdue by a couple of days, so I decided to go to Ed's and pay him. He and Jimmy were sitting on the front porch, so after I paid the rent I sat down and visited with them. I didn't say anything, but I thought old Ed sure looked funny, smoking a handmade cigar stuck in his pipe.

Both Ed and Jimmy seemed glad to see me and asked where I'd been hiding all this time. I told them I'd been busy working and only came to town now when I needed groceries.

I went back on the graveyard shift Sunday night. Raymond had gone home by bus during the weekend to visit his parents and he was tired and sleepy. "I don't know how I'm going to stay awake through this shift," he said. "I haven't had more than two hours sleep the whole weekend. I shouldn't have come to work tonight. You may have to do my job as well as yours."

We began our round of the mine, with me doing most of the work while Raymond waited for me by the rise. When it came time to go to the next level, I talked Raymond into riding the bucket down. He got in and I slowly eased him down with the bit of garbage that was already in it. When he got off, he hollered from the lower level that he'd had a good ride. I walked down and joined him. He rode the bucket all that day, he liked it so much.

When we came to the fifth level, I found some high grade that looked so nice I couldn't resist the temptation. I began to gather some and put it in my bag, piece after piece of it. By the time I had well over ten pounds of high high-grade ore, I became afraid Raymond might notice that my bag was a lot heavier than usual, so I stopped. Before letting Raymond down to the last level, I told him he could load the lorry with the refuse and head for the station, that I had to go to the john and would join him later.

He wouldn't have to wait long for me because I had learned how to come down the ladders quickly. My method was even faster than riding the bucket. I'd place my big miner boots on each side of the ladder, grab the back of it to control my speed, and just slide down to the next landing. I'd come down so fast that sometimes I had to wait on the last landing to see Raymond's light disappear in the drift below.

I came to the crosscut, found a safe spot to hide the high grade and was back at the station before Raymond could get suspicious. We sat on the bench and waited for the cage. Raymond was glad he had showed up for his shift after all, and thanked me for helping him out.

Joe was gone for three days and when he came back he was so sick he couldn't even hold a cup of tea to his mouth; his hands were trembling so bad he'd spill it all over the table. His eyes were red as ripe tomatoes and he looked like he hadn't eaten a thing since he left. His face was drawn and pale, like a very sick old man.

"It was nice to see my family again," he said, "but I got so sick on my way back I thought I'd die. I was hungry, so I stopped at a small store to buy a piece of baloney and it must have been bad. I guess I have a bit of food poisoning and it's going to take a few days to get it out of my system."

I made Joe a pot of rabbit and barley soup and told him to take my bed and stay there until he recovered. I didn't need my bed until I got back from work after eight in the morning anyway.

A couple of days later, when Joe was over his so-called food poisoning, he told me about his visit home. One of his brothers-in-law from Montreal had come for a visit. He owns a tobacco store and a pool hall in Montreal and he wants to sell it. His wife doesn't like the city and wants to move to the country.

"He offered to sell it to me for only four thousand dollars because I'm family," said Joe. "He would ask a lot more from an outsider." Joe's eyes got that wistful look. "That's the kind of business I've always dreamed of owning. I sure wish I had the money to buy him out; I'd be set for life then. But I might be able to when we sell our gold. I'd even have money left over to start my boy in a taxi business as well. I only have to wait for a little while longer."

Although I was tempted to tell Joe about my cache, I thought I'd keep quiet for awhile yet.

Joe had been back from Rouyn for only a few days and was just getting his health back when he mentioned he wanted to go to Kirkland Lake to look for a job. He had heard about a construction company that was building a big mill at one of the mines and he thought he might be able to find a job there. Again he asked if I could lend him five dollars, which I reluctantly did, after telling him that I couldn't keep on lending him money. He said it was very degrading for him to have to ask, but after all, it was just a loan and he was going to repay me as soon as possible.

Joe left that afternoon and was gone for three days. He came back looking ill again, but he wasn't shaking quite so badly this time. He said the job hadn't started yet, but he had talked to one of the bosses who told him to come back in a couple of weeks and he might have a job for him then. He added that he had met a friend who repaid him twelve dollars he had borrowed a long time ago. He took his wallet out and handed me the ten dollars he had borrowed, plus fifty cents I had given him to buy tobacco and cigarette paper. I didn't like to take the fifty cents, but he insisted.

"Now," he said, "tomorrow I'm going to go to Kearns and see about my job in the logging camp, to find out if and when they are going to re-open the camp."

On my job, I kept stashing high-grade ore every day and it was accumulating at a fast rate. It had become almost like a game to me, knowing I was fooling Raymond, who didn't suspect it was odd of me having to go to the john every day at the end of the shift. And sort of playing a game with Joe at the same time by not telling him what I was doing. He would surely be surprised when I told him I had well over a hundred pounds of high grade stashed away in the crosscut.

Joe was gone for five days, explaining when he returned that he had been staying at the camp alone all this time, waiting for one of the bosses to show up, but he hadn't see anyone.

I couldn't keep my secret any longer. I told Joe I had a good lot of high-grade ore hidden safely in the crosscut where I was sure no one would ever find it, even if they took some of the timbers away.

Joe nearly fell off his chair. His face changed from the grim look he had returned with, to a happy smile, and he couldn't wait to ask, "How much have you got stashed?"

"I'm not sure exactly, but there's getting to be a fair amount and my partner doesn't have a clue about it. I don't intend to stop until I have a huge load for you to pack out of there."

Joe got up and began to pace back and forth and I could see he was thinking deeply. "Maybe, if you get enough," he said, "both of us can make the trip down. It's not going to be any harder for the two of us to get into the mine than just one, and we could pack a lot more out that way. What do you think?"

I repeated my reluctance to get involved in the actual stealing of the gold out of the mine. I was very afraid of getting caught and sent to jail.

Joe sat down and slowly went over his plan with me again, emphasizing that it was impossible for us to get caught by anyone during the darkness of the night. "If I thought there was the least chance of us getting caught," he said, "I wouldn't even think of pulling this off. I don't want to go to jail, either, you know What would my family think of me? No sir, it's like I said before, it's as easy as taking candy from a baby."

Still not convinced, I told Joe "I'll keep on doing what I'm doing now and see how I feel about it later."

One afternoon I came back from the mine with my first paycheque. I would be working the rest of the week and would have no time to cash it, so Joe said if I endorsed the check he would cash it in town the next day and pick up a few groceries. He did so and brought me back the right change.

After awhile, he asked, "How much high grade do you have now?"

"Well over one hundred pounds."

"I told you I can't pack more than one hundred pounds," he said, shaking his head. "It would be a shame to have to leave some of it down there. I suppose I could get my friend from Rouyn to give me a hand packing the rest up, but then we'd have to split three ways. I wish you would come down with me. We have nine hundred feet to climb and the air is so much thinner underground and I'm not used to it like you are. I'm going to have to stop and rest on the way up and there won't be much time to spare."

What Joe was saying was sensible. He was only thinking about what was best for us, and besides, I didn't like the idea of splitting the gold three ways any more than he did. His plan seemed safe and everything would probably work out fine. Making up my mind at last, I told him I'd take the chance and go with him. Was he happy to hear that!

"Now you're talking," he said, "I was hoping you'd change your mind. You know, you've put in a lot of hard work and it would be a shame to have to share with someone else just because he made one trip to help pack the stuff out."

As I had said, splitting the money three ways didn't appeal to me, nor did the idea of getting someone else involved. The fewer people who knew about our scheme, the better.

Joe was happy that I had decided to go with him. Pacing back and forth again, he said, "We had better get ready to make a move because we have a lot of preparations to make. We'll only have one shot at this and we don't want to mess it up."

He looked at me to make sure I was listening. "First of all, you'll have to loan me twenty dollars so I can get started. I'll have to go back to Rouyn and borrow a car from a friend. Pete's an old drunk, but he's a real good friend of mine. If I go to his house with a couple of bottles of whiskey, he won't mind lending me his car for a couple of days."

Nodding in agreement, I handed Joe a twenty. "I'll repay you soon," he said.

I would need two days to get ready myself: one to quit my job and one to pick up my check and cash it in town. Then I'd have to pack my belongings, clean up the cabin, and see old Ed to return the key to the cabin and tell him I was moving. It would be a busy couple of days. And beneath all this planning there was a big knot of misgiving settling in my stomach. What had I gotten myself into?

CHAPTER IX

Before leaving for town the next day, Joe told me I should quit my job right away so we wouldn't waste any time when he came back. "I can borrow the car for only so long," he said.

I couldn't bring myself to quit, so I worked my usual shift, stashing more gold. The "game" I was playing was such fun it almost seemed a shame to quit, but I knew I had to. All day I thought of how best to break the news, but nothing I thought of made sense. As we all got out of the cage at the end of the shift, I handed my badge to Ernie and it just came out of my mouth: "This is my last shift, I'm quitting. Could I have my cheque tomorrow afternoon?"

He looked taken aback and asked why I was quitting such an easy job. I lied and said my dad was sick and needed my help on the farm.

"In that case," Ernie said, "I'll turn your time in and your cheque should be ready tomorrow afternoon."

On my way home I though of how easy it had been to quit after all, and I could have kicked myself for having worked that last shift that could put a bug in Joe's plan if I didn't get my cheque in time.

The next day I left the cabin at exactly one o'clock to pick up my cheque. If it wasn't ready, I thought, I'd have something to worry about. But the check was there and I went to town and cashed it, then saw old Ed and returned the key. I didn't go to see Jimmy because I would have to lie to him about why I was leaving Kearns and I didn't want to do that.

The afternoon was spent picking up my rabbit snares, cleaning the cabin and packing my belongings so I would be ready to leave when Joe got back. I expected him that evening, but he didn't return until late the next day, looking tired.

"Have you got the car?" I asked.

"Yep," he said, "and everything else we need."

He showed me the big flashlight he had borrowed and said he had a plank and a length of rope hidden by the road. We'd pick that up on our way to the mine.

"I'm going to lie down and have a good rest," he said. "If I happen to go to sleep, wake me up at ten o'clock. We want to be at the fence no later than eleven. It's dark enough by then to take a reading on the watchman."

"Where's the car?"

"It's by the fence already."

Eager to get going, I woke Joe up at nine thirty. He brewed a pot of tea and smoked a couple of cigarettes. Before we left, we made sure the cabin was spotless.

"Let's grab our packsacks and get going," said Joe. "We've waited long enough for this; we might as well get it over with."

We walked to the mine, stopping at the road to pick up the plank and rope. Then we hurried on down to the big pine tree where I could see the car, well hidden in the weeds, about thirty feet from a dirt road. We were slowly approaching the fence when we saw the watchman with his back toward us punching the time clock. He soon disappeared down a small incline on his way to the next clock. After he left, we placed our gear by the tree and Joe suggested we wait until the watchman came around again before going over the fence. The ground was fairly well illuminated by powerful lights atop tall poles and I had seen that the watchman was carrying something across his shoulders. I asked Joe what it was.

He answered calmly, "A rifle."

Oddly enough, I wasn't as nervous as I thought I would be. I just sat waiting for the watchman and was happy to see him return, whistling a tune.

Joe got to his feet. "Okay," he said. "Let's go. It's about twelve thirty now; we should be back in about two hours."

I climbed the fence first, hoisted myself onto the huge tree limb, and crawled along the limb until I was well over the fence. Tying the rope to the limb, I let myself down to the big rock below. Joe came immediately after and handed me the plank, which I laid alongside the rock to use as a ramp to get ourselves to the ground.

"You make a run for the raise," Joe said in a low voice, "and wait for me a few steps down the ladder."

I ran as fast as I could, opened the door quickly and stepped in. I found myself standing on a small platform from where I could look down at the black hole below me. The ladders were almost horizontal, not like the ones I was able to climb down so fast–those had about a fifteen degree lean.

Joe came in, panting, and said, "Let's get down there as fast as we can."

It wasn't easy getting around with only a light at the landing below. We came to the next level and Joe took the lead for the rest of the way. At the sixth level, he stopped in order to orient himself. He wasn't sure in which direction to go from there, and I couldn't help him because I had never been that far past the crosscut. Finally he made a decision and turned to his right.

We had walked about two hundred feet when we came to a solid wooden door blocking the drift. "Now I know how to find the crosscut," said Joe, and we turned back and went the other way. I was starting to worry, thinking Joe had gotten lost, when we came to a timber pile. I showed Joe the cache and he began to inspect the high grade piece by piece, carefully placing the best pieces in his packsack while I stood by, waiting anxiously. I was getting cold and I was getting worried. He was wasting too much time inspecting the ore.

Finally Joe tested the weight of his packsack and said, "That's about as much as I can pack." Then he filled mine with about forty to sixty pounds.

I noticed the light was fading. "Joe," I said, "we'd better get going with what we've got; the batteries are getting low." He nodded and tossed me my packsack.

Before we even came to the drift, the light had gone out and we were in total darkness. We made our way slowly down the drift by feeling the rails with our feet to make sure we were in the middle and weren't about to bump into one of the walls.

After walking a short distance, Joe stopped and said, "We must be getting close to the rise, but how are we going to know it? Let's walk in the ditch and keep a hand on the wall so we can feel for the widening of the drift. That's about the only way we will ever find the rise."

It was so dark Joe could have been six inches ahead of me and I wouldn't have seen him. Finally he said that he had found it, and when I heard his voice I knew he was about twenty feet from me. I walked a bit faster to catch up and we began the long climb back, wasting a lot of time because between each level we had to feel our way to the next rise.

Time flew by and it wasn't long before we both began to worry. It was obvious that Joe was getting tired; we had to stop and rest every so often because his load was much too heavy.

On the last set of ladders, Joe told me to take the lead and to be very quiet because we didn't know where the watchman might be. I was to wait until he had gone by and was a good distance away before getting out of the rise.

Upon reaching the top, I quietly took off my packsack and put it on the platform while Joe waited a few steps below me. He carefully handed me his packsack and I put it beside mine, then lay flat on my stomach, one eye peering through a crack in the door. To my horror, I could see it was daylight.

Not knowing just where the watchman was, it was with some relief that I heard whistling coming from a few feet away. The watchman walked by, punched the clock, and then turned his back to me and leaned against the door while he lit a cigarette. After he left, I counted slowly to twenty-five before opening the door a crack. He was just disappearing down the incline.

"It's safe," I told Joe. "I'm going to make a run for it," and I did so almost as I spoke.

I ran the sixty feet to the big rock, then up the ramp, tossing my packsack over the fence. As I was climbing up the rope, I could see Joe running toward the rock as fast as he could. Jumping the fifteen feet to the ground, I picked up my packsack and threw it into the car. That's when Joe almost got shot crawling along the limb of the tree.

We got the car going and about three miles past Kearns, Joe slowed down a bit and made a right turn. When we came to a side road, he turned onto it and after driving a few hundred yards he stopped.

"My friend's car is hidden here," Joe said. "I didn't want to take it all the way to the mine in case something went wrong, so I left it here and borrowed this one from a sleeping owner who had left the doors unlocked. You put the packsacks and the rest of our gear in that car while I warm it up."

Sensing my hesitation, Joe shouted, "Hurry up! The cops should be getting ready for a chase about now."

It took only a couple of minutes for me to transfer the high grade and our gear. Now I was the one who was in a hurry. "Come on, Joe, get going," I said as I pitched the last of our belongings into the car.

He waited a minute or two longer, in order to warm up the motor, and then he took off, driving like a desperado. He scared the life out of me; my head was hitting the roof as he sped around curves and over bumps. I didn't dare let go of the door handle so I could look at the odometer and check the speed we were going.

A few miles down the road we came to the small town of Arntfield—one store, a gas pump and a few scattered houses. Joe didn't even slow down. "We're twelve miles from Rouyn," he said. "If we can make the next six miles without a cop chasing us, we're safe."

Four or five miles past Arntfield, Joe began to slow down. A short while later he said, "You see that leaning telephone pole ahead?"

"Yes."

"I'm going to stop there and as soon as I stop you grab the packsacks and dump them in the ditch. Make sure they are well covered by water so nobody can see them."

The car was still moving when I jumped out. I grabbed the big packsack first, ran to the ditch and lowered it into the water, then did the same thing to the other one. Noticing the stem of a big cattail nearby, I picked it up and placed it near the edge of the ditch as a marker, pointing between the two packsacks.

When I got back to the car Joe said "We're only going to that old abandoned farm there," and he pointed to his left. Over the tall weeds, I could see a big barn and a small log house about one hundred feet away.

Joe didn't want to go down the driveway. He said it might look suspicious if the cops happened to drive by and see fresh tire marks turning in. He parked on the road, got out of the car, and we unloaded our gear, tossing everything as far as we could up the driveway. As he got back into the car, Joe said, "You stay here. "I'll be back as soon as I've returned the car; and I'll bring the equipment we'll need to process the high grade." Then he was off in a cloud of dust.

I took two of the packsacks that held our belongings and walked up to the old house. It was in a bad state of repair: the porch was tilted to one side, the windows had been removed, and the door was gone. When I went in, I could smell mice, and the floor was littered with their droppings. I sincerely hoped we wouldn't have to stay there for very long.

Tossing the packsacks in a corner, I trudged back to get the rest of our gear, but when I saw a cloud of dust up the road, I grabbed what I could, hurried back and hid behind the house. As the car went by, I peeked around the corner of the house and could see spelled out in large letters, O.P.P. I knew it was a police car because I had seen one just like it, with the same kind of lights on the roof, in Virginia Town.

When I thought it was safe, I got the rest of our gear and hid it a few feet from the house, then sat on the ground near the road to regain my composure. My hands were shaking. I was scared now that the police were involved.

During the next two hours, I moved only once, to raise my head above the weeds when I heard the sound of a car. It was the same police car, this time heading back toward Ontario. This made me feel a bit safe, seeing the police returning after taking care of whatever business they had in Rouyn.

Feeling a little calmer, I realized I was famished. Luckily, I had brought almost all the food I had in my cabin, and there was lots of it. I wouldn't run out of food for a long time. A piece of bread and bologna satisfied my hunger and I was ready to look around the place.

Walking behind the old house I saw a big pile of firewood, a well and, a few feet away, a bucket, still hanging at the end of a rope from a roller. I sent the bucket down and got some water that really tasted good.

That day at the old abandoned farm was the longest of my life–hiding among the weeds near the road, just waiting for Joe to come back and not knowing what to expect next. I raised my head a little whenever I heard a vehicle passing by (which was very seldom). My mind was preoccupied with all sorts of problems and I could come up with no solution to any of them.

Night was coming quickly and I was beginning to get very cold. I didn't want to sleep on the floor of the smelly old house and I had only one blanket with me, which wouldn't keep me warm on a cold night in early October. As much as I hated to, I'd have to light a fire. Choosing the driest wood I could find so it wouldn't make too much smoke that might be seen from the road, I made a small fire and brewed a pot of tea. After having something to eat, I dozed off.

A voice woke me up during the night and I almost jumped out of my sin. "Where are you?" asked the voice, and it took me awhile to realize it was Joe.

I got up, cold and shivering. "I'm here," I said as I walked in the direction of the voice. "What's going on?"

"I didn't want anyone to see me come up this way," said Joe. "I had to wait until dark and then hide in the bushes a couple of times when I saw headlights on the road. It took me a long time to get here, but I made it and I brought the gear we need to process the high grade. You can start tomorrow morning, using this pipe." He handed it to me and then showed me another instrument. "Use this as a hammer to crush the rock after you place one or two pieces in the pipe. It works good." Then he handed me a newspaper. "Save the fines on this, and I'll come and work with you as soon as I can."

Joe sounded almost as scared as I was, probably because he had been playing hide and seek with the cops on the road, but he tried to be reassuring. "I have a friend who has a taxi in town," he said. "I asked him to keep an ear open and tell me if he hears anything about a gold robbery in one of the mines in this area. Rodger is safe; he wouldn't blab to anyone."

After talking with Joe for nearly an hour, I felt a bit better. At least I knew he was trying his best to get us through this situation.

By now I was too cold to go back to sleep so I decided to light a small fire in order to get warmed up. After eating some more bologna, washed down with cold water, I sat by the fire and eventually fell asleep that way–sitting on the cold ground. I awoke at dawn to a cold and windy day.

Feeling much bolder, I made a big fire the way Dad had showed me on the trapline. There was no birch bark available so I used some dry grass for kindling, then heaped on dry wood until I had a cone-shaped pile. The dry grass took at once and soon I had a good fire going, with little smoke because of the dryness of the wood.

After a big breakfast of crepes, I went to the ditch and retrieved the smaller of the two packsacks containing ore. Sitting on the broken-down porch, I began the job of crushing the high grade. First I poured about two inches of ore into the pipe, which was a foot-and-a-half long and two inches across, with a metal plate welded on the bottom. Then I took the special rod or hammer, which was one-and-one-half inches across and fitted easily into the pipe, and began pounding, with an up and down motion. It was necessary to check now and then to see if I had crushed the ore fine enough and, when I thought I had, I'd dump the fines on a sheet of newspaper and put the bigger pieces to one side.

I kept at it for most of the day, until my arm ached from pulverizing the rocks, but in the end I had a big pile of sand waiting for Joe to do whatever had to be done next.

While I was working, I had kept a sharp eye on the traffic but didn't see anything unusual, so I began to relax. Joe came back long after dark, walking across farmers' fields and through bushes. He seemed very nervous and upset. His friend at the taxi stand, Rodger Belcour, had told him that the news about the robbery was out. In fact, it was all over town that the cops knew the vehicle involved in the robbery had been traveling toward Rouyn and they were quite certain the robbers were still in the surrounding area, but no big scale search had been mentioned.

We talked for a long time, sitting in the dark in the freezing cold. "You carry on crushing and tomorrow I'll come up and start washing," Joe said. It won't take me long to wash everything. I'll bring some cans or jars to put the gold in, too. If we could get finished in three or four days, it would be just great. I'm trying to make arrangements with Rodger to drive us to Toronto and I hope we can come to an understanding. Try not to light a fire any more," he cautioned. "Even if they can't see the smoke, they can smell it a long ways away and someone might report it."

Up again at dawn, I ate bread and bologna for breakfast, washed it down with cold water, and went to work. Sitting on the front porch all day, I raised and lowered that hammer with all the power I had. By nightfall, the smaller packsack was empty.

Joe came early the next morning, bringing me a thermos of hot coffee and a blanket. He knew it was cold and that it was a hardship for me to have to sleep outside and drink only cold water with my meals.

Having retrieved the larger packsack after dark the previous evening, I bought it up onto the porch, but before beginning work, I watched Joe. He had arrived a bit earlier and wasn't wasting any time. I watched him pan the sand and pick up the bigger pieces, dumping them into a tall tin can. At the end of the day the can was nearly full of beautiful, glistening gold. The can was so heavy I could barely lift it.

Joe left again that night and didn't come back for three days. The first day I didn't think much of it, but just kept working, expecting him to show up at any time. But when he didn't show up for three days in a row I really began to worry, afraid something had happened to him.

The blackest thoughts started to form in my mind. Knowing he was a sick man, I asked myself if his ulcer could have erupted and he was lying dead somewhere in the bush between Rouyn and the farm. Or had the cops arrested him and he was sitting in jail at this moment, implicating me in the robbery? By the third day I was so worried I was unable to work.

Leaving around noon, I went for a long walk across the field and into the forest, not returning until dark. It was a really cold night, with a strong northeastern wind blowing, so I decided to brave the smell of the old house and sleep on the floor. At least there I was protected from the wind and, hopefully, I would get to sleep before the vile odour of the rodents made me sick. Still worried, I was afraid I wouldn't be able to sleep, but I was so tired that I had my best night's sleep since the robbery.

I was freezing when I woke up, but I didn't stand still long enough to even think about it. After checking the amount of high grade that was left, I was sure I could be finished in two more days.

I had been working for no more than an hour when Rodger dropped Joe off. Joe's brows were curled down and his forehead creased. He was obviously worried and seemed to be deep in thought. Joe was never very talkative and I had to drag every word out of him at first, but then he opened up.

"I might as well tell you the whole story," he said, "because you'll probably find out sooner or later. First of all, I never told you the truth about why I couldn't work in mines any more. I got fired from Kerr Addison for trying to steal gold and I was blackballed from the gold mines. Now, I guess, my name has come up as a suspect in this robbery and they caught up with me."

My heart was beating fast now. "What happened?"

"I was picked up by the cops and taken down to the police station for interrogation, grilled for over three hours and then released. I wanted to come and tell you what had happened, but I was afraid they might be watching me. Anyways, it was too late to come up that day, so I thought I'd tell you about it the next day. But they picked me up again the next morning as I was leaving to come here. They took me down for more questioning and this time they locked me up and kept me in a cell overnight. I wasn't released until late the next afternoon."

"So, everything's okay?"

"Well, I'm sure they're done with me. They've asked me just about every question they could think of, and I answered every one of them to their satisfaction. They don't have a thing on me, but they would like to ask you a few questions if they ever find you, because I had to tell them I was staying at your place. I had no other choice."

That didn't sit too well with me, but Joe didn't seem to notice. He went on talking, but by now he was bragging.

"I'm too smart for them. When they released me the first day, I phoned a lady I know in Kirkland Lake and told her to say, if anyone called and asked her my whereabouts for the first week of October, that I was staying at her place and I only left the house for a couple of hours to go to town a few times during that week." He smiled proudly. "That's why they kept me in jail that one night. They couldn't get her on the phone. Now they've talked with her, I'm sure they won't bother me any more."

Joe seemed to feel better after having unloaded on me, and he began to wash the gold.

There was not much I could do about what had happened, so I went back to crushing the rest of the high grade and it wasn't long before I was finished. That left Joe with about one more day of washing the rest of the sand and we'd be ready for the next step, which was to sell the gold.

Rodger had agreed to drive us to Toronto and take us to a man he was sure would buy everything we had. Rodger said he had made quite a few trips to sell gold to the man and would charge us only two hundred dollars. I didn't know a thing about taxi fares, but according to Joe it was a good deal.

When Joe was finished, we had six cans full of gold dust, with many nice big nuggets showing among the finer grains of gold. After testing the approximate weight of each can, Joe said we had well over sixty pounds of gold dust, which should bring us more than twenty thousand dollars.

Once again, Joe thanked me. "I'm going to have enough money to buy my pool hall and have plenty left over, even after starting my son in a taxi business in Montreal."

Joe waited until fairly late in the afternoon for Rodger to pick him up in his taxi to return to Rouyn. (Joe didn't want to sleep outside for even one night, or in the smelly house, either.) He told me to have the cans in the packsacks and to be ready to leave for Toronto as soon as they got there. They planned to arrive early in the morning because it was a long drive.

CHAPTER X

The excitement of seeing my first big city was mingled with fear, so I barely slept a wink that night. On top of that was my confusion over what I was going to do with all that money. I couldn't even conceive of how big a stack it would make, except that I was fairly sure it wouldn't fit into my hip pocket. It would have to go into my packsack, and I would have to keep it on my back so nobody could steal it and so I didn't forget it somewhere. My mind was so active, it wouldn't let my body sleep.

When daylight came I felt tired and would have gladly delayed our trip to get a few more hours sleep, but I didn't have much choice in the matter. Forcing myself to get up, I knelt down and took the six cans of gold out from under the floor boards where I had hidden them the night before. I put the cans into the two packsacks and hid the sacks in the tall weeds by the road.

A few minutes later I heard a car and immediately jumped up, and just as quickly sat down again. It was a small truck, moving very slowly. I was terrified it would stop at the entrance of the driveway just as Joe got there with the taxi, but the truck went past at the same slow speed.

Just as the truck disappeared I heard the sound of another car and this time it was the taxi, traveling at a high speed. When it ground to a stop at the driveway, Joe jumped out, took the packsacks and waited until Rodger opened the trunk so he could toss them inside.

There was something different about the car, so I asked Joe if it was the same one he had been using.

"Yeah, it's the same, but what with the gas rationing, taxis aren't allowed to go more than fifteen miles outside the city limits, so Rodger took off the taxi sign and repainted the doors."

This exchange appeared to annoy Rodger and I heard him say in a low voice to Joe, "Why is he asking so many questions? He has nothing to worry about and we don't owe him any explanations. The less he knows, the better off we are."

I wasn't sure what was going on between the two of them, but it sounded like something was brewing. If I had taken that as a warning and followed my suspicions, I would have saved myself a whole lot of trouble, but I shrugged it off. We all got in the car and I was so tired I leaned back in my seat and was soon asleep.

I woke up to see Joe getting out of the car. Rodger was telling him not to be too long with his girlfriend because we still had a lot of driving to do and we shouldn't waste any time. I wanted to ask Rodger where we were, but I didn't dare because I knew he didn't like me much. Instead, I just leaned back in the seat and pretended I was still asleep.

Joe came back in a few minutes, saying, "Judy doesn't want to move to Montreal."

Rodger didn't answer; he just got the car moving and turned onto a street where the traffic was fairly heavy.

Still half asleep, I opened one eye and looked out the side window. We went by a sign that read, Kirkland Lake, and there was a mine, almost in the middle of town. When we got out of town, Rodger put his foot on the accelerator and we traveled at a high speed on a road bordered by forest on both sides, with no signs of civilization. I leaned back and went to sleep again.

When I awoke, I could hear Rodger saying, "I haven't seen any of that yellow stuff yet, but if you have as much of it as you say, I'm sure you'll get more than twenty thousand. As I told you before, my friend pays twenty dollars an ounce for good clean dust. If he likes your stuff, you should get well over twenty thousand dollars." When I moved, Rodger stopped talking.

I sat up and looked out the window. We were entering a fairly large city, and moving at a much slower speed than before. A sign by the road said, Welcome to North Bay! Rodger drove slowly along what looked like the main street, apparently looking for a particular place. Finally, Joe said, "Right here," and Rodger stopped.

Joe turned to me and asked, "Can you lend me a ten? Our friend, here, is thirsty."

I had a ten in my watch pocket, so I pulled it out and handed it to him. "I owe you twenty now," he said. "You know you'll get it back soon. No problem."

When Joe came out of the store he was holding a brown paper bag. As soon as he got back in the car Rodger drove off and before long we were out of the city. Joe opened two bottles of beer and handed one to Rodger. I was disappointed because I had thought Joe went to the store to buy something to eat. It was getting late in the day and I had had an early breakfast; now I was hungry.

I was afraid to ask Rodger to stop again in order to buy food, in case he got mad, so I just tried to forget my hunger. As I leaned my head against the cushion, the smell of beer drifted back to me. It was the same smell I had detected on Joe's breath back in the cabin when he had returned home sick, he had said, from food poisoning. It hadn't been food poisoning, I realized now; he had been drinking.

By the time the two of them were through their third bottle of beer, they began to talk louder and to slur their words. I began to worry that Rodger might get too drunk to drive.

Joe said something to Rodger that I didn't hear, and Rodger replied, "It wasn't that at all. Your trouble was strictly booze. If you had left it alone, you'd still be in business today."

Joe didn't like Rodger's comment, but he didn't say anything more. He turned to me, holding out his beer. "Here, kid, have a drink. You must be thirsty by now."

I turned down the beer, but by this time I was so hungry I had to say something. "I'm not thirsty," I told Joe, "but I sure am hungry. I haven't had anything to eat since early this morning. Could we stop at a store and buy some food?"

"Yeah," said Joe, turning to Rodger. "We have to feed this kid. We can't let him die of starvation."

Further down the road we came to a gas pump near a small store. Rodger pulled in and while he was filling up, Joe went to the store, coming back with bologna, cookies and pop. He handed me the food and Rodger got the car back on the road, driving at neck-breaking speed.

After eating my fill I went back to sleep and when I awoke it was dark and Rodger was driving much slower. This was no small town; I could see street lights and neon signs flashing by and I knew we were entering Toronto. I was excited and I wanted to say something to Joe, but his head was tilted forward onto his chest as if he were asleep.

It seemed as though we had been driving for a long time when Rodger yelled at Joe to wake up. He handed Joe a notebook and told him to look up the address of Archie Bushner, saying he thought we were getting fairly close to his place.

Flipping through a few pages, Joe found the address and read it to Rodger.

"Damn," said Rodger. "We've gone past." He made a turn and soon we were on a side street and about half an hour later he stopped in front of a big red brick house with a high steel fence around the yard. Rodger went up to the gate and spoke into the intercom, and after getting an affirmative reply he motioned to Joe to come with him.

They had been gone nearly a half an hour when I saw Joe come around the corner from the back of the house. He came directly to the car, opened the trunk and took one packsack out, then returned to the house. It was a long time before the two of them returned. Joe threw the packsack in the trunk and they both got into the car.

"We might as well drive around and see if we can find a place to spend the rest of the night," said Rodger.

Afraid to ask questions, I just sat and listened to the two of them talking. Rodger finally said something that made me understand why we had to spend the rest of the night in Toronto. The man didn't have that much money in the house. He'd have to go to the bank in the morning to get enough money to buy the gold dust. The good news was that he was definitely going to buy it.

We drove for nearly an hour before Rodger spotted a rather small hotel with a dimly-lighted sign that said: Rooms to Let. He said to Joe, "We might as well go in and get ourselves a room here. It might not be that nice of a place, but it's close to Archie's house and I don't feel like driving too far into the city."

Joe told me I should stay in the car to make sure it wasn't stolen, that I would be just fine sleeping on the back seat.

I watched them going into the building and realized that I wasn't at all sleepy. I had slept for a few hours during the trip and now I was feeling hyper, like taking off down the street and running like a deer. Certainly I was tired of sitting, but I didn't dare get out of the car, afraid that I might get lost in such a big city and not be able to find the car again. Toward morning I finally went to sleep and didn't wake up until I heard Rodger unlock the car door. They had both eaten breakfast, but Joe brought me some toast and jam that I ate while we drove back to Archie's place.

We had been driving for some time when Joe told Rodger to stop as we were coming to a store. "We have plenty of time; it's not eleven o'clock yet. I want to buy our kid here something to eat. I'm sure he's still hungry."

It was funny to hear Joe calling me a kid. In all the time we had spent together, he had never called me that.

When we got to the store, Joe asked me what I wanted to drink with my bologna. "If they sell milk, buy me some, I said.

As son as Joe got back, Rodger drove straight to the big brick house and parked at the front. He and Joe talked into the intercom and then walked around the back, taking the packsacks with them. They were in there for a long time before coming out again, joking and laughing. The packsacks looked a lot lighter. They put the sacks in the trunk and got in the car without saying a word.

Rodger began driving in the direction we had come from, neither of them saying anything. I couldn't stand the suspense any longer. "How much money did we get?" I asked Joe.

Without turning his head, he said in a dry voice, "Twenty thousand nine hundred dollars." He glanced at Rodger, who didn't return the look but kept on driving until we were out of the city. Since neither of them seemed inclined to talk, and the ride was smooth, I found myself nodding off again. The trip was becoming monotonous and I'd be happy to see it end.

It was easy to tell when we were getting close to North Bay. There were more houses on both sides of the road and the traffic was increasing.

A few miles before entering the city we came to a paved road and Rodger spoke for the first time. "Joe, I'm too tired to drive any farther today. We're going to get a room here and stay the night."

"You're going to have to stay in the car again tonight to keep an eye on things," Joe said to me. "I'm going to the store and get you something to eat, but you'll have to give me some money. I only have a dollar left from the ten you loaned me."

I reached in my side pocket, came out with a two-dollar bill and asked Joe if that was enough.

"Yes," said Joe as he got out of the car. "I'll be back in a few minutes."

Joe came back, handed me a bag of groceries, and warned me not to get out of the car because I'd have to leave it unlocked and it could get stolen. "We have too much money in the trunk to take that chance," he said. "Keep your head down as much as possible, too. There could be cops walking the streets at night and if they see you, they might come over and ask you questions and we don't want that, either." With that last warning, he headed for the hotel to join Rodger.

In the bag Joe left me there was a loaf of bread, a pound of butter, two chocolate bars, some sliced ham, a quart of milk and a bottle of pop. After consuming the chocolate bars I was full, so I settled back in the seat and went to sleep.

A short while later the sound of loud laughter awakened me. Raising my head slowly to look out the window, I saw Joe and Rodger standing on the sidewalk in front of the hotel. It was plain to see they had been drinking. A taxi pulled up and they staggered over to it and got in.

I watched the taxi pull away and then, realizing I was hungry, I ate a few slices of ham. I wished I could make myself a sandwich, but my knife was in the packsack, locked up in the trunk. I had a drink of milk and lay down again, trying to get back to sleep, but I felt restless and wished I knew what time it was. Grabbing the back of the seat to help myself get to the sitting position, I pulled the seat loose and it fell forward, enabling me to see inside the trunk. I could see the packsacks and all our other belongings through the gap. I reached in to get the packsack that held my hunting knife, so I could make a sandwich, but when I pulled the packsack out and opened it, there was all that money staring at me. I pulled out a big stack of one hundred-dollar bills and could see that there was another stack of hundreds, plus a couple of stacks of fifties and some twenties, all tied with an elastic band. Hurriedly, I replaced the packsack and reached for the bigger one, which held my hunting knife.

Seeing all that money made me nervous; I was almost shaking with fright, and worried, too, that maybe I had damaged Rodger's car. He wouldn't like that. Getting to my knees, I struggled with the back of the seat and eventually got it back on its hooks. It was a relief to see that there was no damage done. No one would even notice it had come apart.

I lay back on the seat again, although wide awake and wondering what time it was. There were fewer footsteps on the sidewalk now and less traffic on the road, so it must be quite late. I tried to get back to sleep but it was difficult with the flashing neon lights and the street lights that shone into the car, making it seem almost like daytime.

Although I still hadn't slept a wink, I was startled by the sound of laughter again. When I raised my head, I could see it was daylight and Joe and Rodger were getting out of a taxi, almost too drunk to walk the few steps to the hotel door. This worried me so much I didn't feel tired or sleepy any more. I wondered if they would be in any condition for us to get away from North Bay that day. Eventually, I got too tired to think anymore and went to sleep. When I woke up, we were on our way and were well out of the city. Joe and Rodger were talking. "I haven't seen Gerome since he went to Montreal and bought the Belmont Hotel on St. Catherine Street," Joe was saying. "And did you know that Henri bought the pool hall and tobacco store just a block from him?"

"I didn't know that," said Rodger. "They are sure going to be surprised to see us when we get there." They stopped talking when I sat up and I could see they each had a bottle of beer and were feeling no pain.

When I looked out the window I didn't recognize the scenery. We weren't going back the way we had come and I didn't know why Rodger had taken a different route, but I didn't ask any questions. A short while later we came to Tamagami, a very small town with one hotel, one store, and only a few houses on each side of the road.

It was getting late in the afternoon, almost dark enough to turn on the headlights, when Joe reached down for another beer and said to Rodger, "We're on our last bottle, you know. We're going to have to stop somewhere and buy another case." He was slurring his words so much I could barely make out what he was saying, and after a few more gulps from his bottle, he went to sleep.

Rodger drove on in silence for quite a while before waking Joe up. "We're going through Cobalt," he said. "It won't be long now before we're in Hilbery so you better be alert. We're going to stop there for a drink and something to eat if we're not too late for the restaurant."

As soon as Joe woke up he reached for his bottle that had spilled on the floor. It had only a little left in it and it was warm, but Joe guzzled it down anyway. He patted his hair down with both hands and said to Rodger, "I'm not hungry, but I could sure go for a good stiff drink."

When we came to Hilibery, another small town, Rodger pulled off the road and drove around the back of a hotel where the sign read: Tavern. He parked and said, "Let's go in." Then Rodger looked at me for the very first time and said, "You come in, too. We're going to be here for awhile and you need to stretch your legs."

I was glad to get out of the car at last, and I needed to go to the bathroom so badly I could hardly hold myself. The last time I had gone was out of the car door just before we left North Bay, and that was only the fifth time in three days.

I was surprised to see how big the tavern was, for a small town, and it was so dark I had a hard time finding my way around. We sat at a table in a far corner and were waited on by a giant of a man, well over six feet, with blond curly hair. He was about twenty years old.

"Bring us three scotches," said Joe.

"Not for me, Joe," I said hurriedly. "I don't drink."

"You're a miner, you have to have a drink with us."

"No," I insisted. "I don't want a drink. I want to use the bathroom and I'll just have a glass of water."

The bartender pointed to the bathroom, saying, "Down the hall, last door to your right."

In the bathroom there was a basin with soap and towels, so I washed my face with cold water. It felt good and helped me to wake up.

When I returned to the table there was a tall glass of what looked like water waiting for me. I took a long drink and discovered that it tasted a bit like some kind of perfume. I didn't like that brand of pop. I set my glass down and watched as Joe and Rodger had a drink of whiskey, followed by a drink of beer All the while they were talking about our trip and how they would be leaving for Montreal in a few days.

Rodger seemed to be getting a little more friendly toward me and began urging me to have another drink. "Hurry and finish your drink," he said. "We have to get going soon."

I took a few more sips just to please him and soon I began to feel funny. My brain wasn't working properly; it was kind of fuzzy, and the room seemed to be going around in circles. Through the fuzziness I could hear Rodger telling me to finish my drink, that it would clear my head. Then I lost contact with reality. My head hit the table and the lights went out.

CHAPTER XI

I was very disoriented when I woke up in a strange room, lying on top of the bed with all my clothes on. I had an unbearable headache that I thought would split my head open, and on top of that I was so thirsty I could barely swallow. Not sure that I could even walk, I was afraid to get off the bed so I lay there for at least a half an hour before daring to make a move. Sliding slowly off the bed, I stood on two very shaky legs and managed to go as far as the sink for a drink of water.

Looking in the mirror I almost didn't recognize my own face, it was so puffed up and gray. My eyes were almost as red as Joe's when he had returned to cabin sick. I really wanted to look out the window to see exactly where I was, but my legs were too weak to make it that far. Instead, I stumbled back to the bed and flopped face down.

What could have made me that sick? I couldn't come up with an answer. All I had consumed at the bar was that soda pop and I drank so little surely it couldn't have made me this sick.

After lying on the bed for a long time I decided to force myself to get up and go for a walk in the cold air. That might help me get better more than anything else. Shakily I walked to the bedroom door, opened it and peered up and down the long hallway. There was no one in sight so I ventured out, making my way to the stairs, where I stopped and listened to hear if there was anyone on the main floor. Unable to hear anything, I went down the stairs and out the front door.

The cold air didn't seem to help my headache much as I walked along the shoulder of the highway. Coming to a large culvert, I stood looking at the water cascading down the small stream and decided to wash my face again in the ice cold water. Afterward, climbing the steep bank back to the highway, I noticed an elderly man watching me.

"You must have tied a good one on last night, to go to sleep by this stream," he said.

"I didn't sleep here; I just went down to wash my face. I thought it might help to get rid of my headache."

"Just the same, you must have tied on one if you have a headache."

"I don't drink. I was in a tavern last night with my friends, but all I had to drink was a glass of soda pop. I didn't even finish it because my head got all blurry, the room began to turn, and I fell asleep at the table.

When I woke up this morning with this headache, I couldn't even remember how I got to my room."

The old fellow looked at me sadly. "I think your friends gave you a Mickey Finn."

"What do you mean?"

"They doped you. They put something in your glass to knock you out. I bet they stole your money, too."

Immediately, I felt in my shirt pocket, but my money was still there–at least, one hundred dollars of it was. "No," I said, "I still have my money."

"Well, they didn't do it for nothing, that's for sure. If they gave you some knockout drops, they must have had some reason."

We walked back to town together and when we came to the hotel he said, "Take care of yourself," and he kept on going toward the store.

I came in through the front door and still didn't see anyone. The clock behind the counter showed a quarter after one. Instead of going up the stairs I went into the tavern where the same blond giant was sweeping the floor. Without looking up, he said, "The tavern isn't open yet." Then he looked up and saw me. "Your uncle hasn't been around to pick you up yet?"

"What uncle?"

"Wasn't that your uncle who rented the room for you last night and carried you to bed?"

"No," I said. "I don't have any uncles anywhere near here. I was with some friends last night and all of a sudden I fell asleep for some reason."

"Well, that big burly man told me you were his nephew, that you had been out hunting and were dead tired from the trip. He rented you a room and left with the other man to go visit a friend. He said he was going to come back for you at noon today, but I see it's well past that now. By the way," he added, "he left your packsack behind the counter in the lobby."

I thanked him and went back to the lobby where I sat down and contemplated my next move. I had been slow in sorting things out, but by now I knew I had been double crossed. Joe and Rodger were gone with all the money, including the twenty Joe had borrowed from me. I sat as if in a stupor, not knowing what to do.

It was almost four o'clock when a woman appeared behind the counter and asked if I was waiting for the bus.

"What bus is that?"

"The one heading east. It comes by at four thirty and goes as far as Rouyn."

"How much for a ticket?"

"Three dollars and twenty-five cents."

I bought a ticket and went outside. Sitting on my packsack near the road, I waited with two other men. When the bus came I found a vacant seat where I could sit alone by the window so I could do some thinking. I barely noticed when we took off, nor did the passing scenery hold any interest for me.

"Ville Marie, next stop," called the driver.

My thoughts interrupted, I was looking through the window when we pulled in front of a hotel in Ville Marie and there, before my very eyes, was Rodger's car parked on the street. My first reaction was to confront them both right in the hotel and demand my share of the money, but I forced myself to think before acting. If I confronted them in public there was no way I could mention my share of the money and they would just brush me off. Then, too, they would probably manage to give me the slip again and, knowing I was after them, they would cover their tracks and I might never find them again.

Remaining in my seat, I kept my eyes glued to the hotel until the driver got back on and we began to move. I still didn't have a plan in mind, but when the driver called, "Arntfield, next stop," my brain began to function again. After the driver dropped off a few parcels in Arntfield and we were on the road again, I asked him if he could let me out about three miles down the road.

"I can drop you off anywhere you want. All you have to do is tell me."

I waited up front with my packsack until I saw the leaning telephone pole. I pointed it out to him and said, "That's where I want off."

"No problem," he said, and stopped the bus. I jumped off and was left alone in total darkness.

I walked around to the back of the old farmhouse and sat on my packsack near a big pile of firewood. The headache I had wakened with was still there, but I was able to think clearly for the first time since morning.

One thing that was to my advantage was that I was ahead of them and I might be able to follow their movements when they got to Rouyn. I had to find out what they were going to do with all that money. They wouldn't dare put it in the bank, and if it was left in the truck of the car, sooner or later I would have a chance to get my share.

By now I was hungry, not having had anything to eat all day, which was very unusual for me. As a rule, I had to be really sick to miss even one meal. After building a fire I made some tea and ate two bologna sandwiches. Four cups of strong black tea seemed to assuage my headache and I felt relaxed for the first time since waking up that morning. I bedded down near the fire, getting up a few times during the night to add wood to it.

I woke up at daylight, refreshed but not in any hurry to go anywhere. I was going to wait at the farm until I saw the taxi drive past. Sooner or later they had to get to Rouyn and they would have to go past me to get there.

Most of the day was spent sitting near the road, watching every car that went by. I was quite pleased with myself for having thought of this plan, as I was sure it was a good one.

It was beginning to get dark when I saw Rodger drive by at a fairly slow speed. There was plenty of time for me to get a good look at the two of them, with Joe tilting a bottle of beer to his mouth.

Slipping on my packsack, I began to walk as fast as I could toward Rouyn. I should have no trouble finding them. They would just be nicely settled in one of the taverns by the time I arrived. If I found the car in a dark alley, all I had to do was break a window, remove the back seat and take my money. It sounded so simple, like Joe had once said: as easy as taking candy from baby.

When I got to Rouyn I was surprised to see so many people on Main Street. I was a bit embarrassed to be carrying a packsack at that time of day when most people were settled for the night. I walked all the way to the Commercial Hotel, watching for the car on both sides of the street as well as down the side streets, but it wasn't anywhere around. Crossing the street, I began to look for the Rainbow taxi stand where Rodger worked, finally locating it on a side street, a half block from Main.

Hiding in the shadow of a doorway across from the stand, I kept vigil for nearly a half an hour, hoping I'd see Rodger, but no luck. There was only one man in the small stand, and he hadn't moved his eyes from the book he'd been reading. Finally I went over to the stand and went in.

"Taxi?" he said, reluctantly raising his eyes from the book.

"No. I'm looking for Rodger. Have you seen him tonight?"

"No. Rodger doesn't work here anymore. He quit a few days ago. What do you want to see him about?"

"I want to repay what I owe him."

"Well," he said, "you might have to go to Montreal for that, because he said that's where he was moving to. Since his wife left him he's been drinking a lot; that's why he got fired. I'm sorry I can't help you more."

Wanting to know more about the two men, I asked if he knew Joe Martel.

"Oh, sure. I've known Joe for a long time. He used to work here. Him and Rodger have been friends for years. In fact, it's Rodger that financed Joe to buy a taxi. He worked for us for about four months, then one day when he'd been drinking he hit a woman in a crosswalk and nearly killed her. That's when the boss fired him. His wife was so fed up she threw him out of the house, and Joe began to drink more and more all the time. Now he's a real alcoholic and can't go for very long without his booze."

I thanked him and went back to the main street. As I turned to look at the taxi stand again, there was Rodger's car, parked right in front. Rodger was standing in the doorway, but a few minutes later he got back in the car and drove off.

Hurrying back to the stand, I said, "I guess I just missed Rodger," and I asked if he was going to return.

"No. He and Joe are on their way to Montreal. They're leaving right now. Too bad you missed him."

My plan had failed. Now I'd never have a chance to get back my share of the money. I figured I might as well head for the station and take the freight home, if there was one that night. And I wouldn't mention anything about my escapade to anyone.

About half a mile past the station I got off the tracks and went a few feet up an incline where I would be hidden among the shrubs while I waited for a freight. About an hour later I heard footsteps on the gravel and a man sat down a few feet below me. I saw him light his pipe and soon the fragrant smoke came drifting toward me, reminding me of my dad when he smoked, and making me lonesome for home.

This stranger was waiting for a freight, too, and I might learn something from him, so I walked down to where he was sitting.

He was startled when I said, "Hi."

"Where do you come from?" he asked.

"I've been working in a gold mine and now I'm on my way home, just waiting to catch the first freight that comes by."

He was a small man, much the same size as my dad, but he was well dressed and carried a suitcase. "How far are you going?" he asked.

"Tiblemont," I said. "It's seven miles from Senneterre."

"Oh. I'm going a bit farther than that–to Lassare. My daughter lives there on a farm. Since I've been widowed, I've worked for the forestry, looking after a watchtower a few miles out of Rouyn. I spend the summer there and go back to my daughter's place for the winter. How about you? Are you going home for a visit?"

My mind wasn't made up, so I didn't quite know how to answer. After thinking about it I said, "If I told you something very personal, could you keep it a secret?"

"Oh, yes, I'm sure I could. A stranger is always the best person to tell a secret to because if he repeats it, the person who told the secret never gets to know about it and it remains a secret."

That explanation eluded me, but I decided to confide in him anyway. I told him I had stolen some gold from a mine, and then went on with the rest of the story about how I had been double-crossed by my friend and that he was on his way to Montreal with my share of the money.

He listened patiently to my tale of woe and then spoke with seeming sincerity. "You can't let them get away with that. You have to go after them. Go to Montreal. You know they're going to the Belmont Hotel and you won't have any trouble finding it. With a tongue in your head you can find anything you want. Montreal is a big city, but you'll find that most people like to give out information and if those two were drinking when they left, chances are they're going to carry on drinking until all that money is gone."

He became quite insistent. "You go to Montreal. Get off this freight at Senneterre and grab the next one to take you on your way. If I were your age, I'd never give up on something like this. You'll find out how good it feels to get even with someone who thinks he has outsmarted you. Take my advice and you won't regret it."

Around midnight a freight came along and we both jumped on. We were on our way.

He didn't talk much after that, except to tell me he had ridden freights so many times during the depression that now it was his favourite mode of transportation.

Before parting in Senneterre he told me I should wait for the next freight by the water tank–about a mile past the station. That way I'd have plenty of time to find a boxcar because the freight would stop there for at least fifteen minutes to load up with water.

As I came near the water tank I noticed an older man sitting on the edge of the tracks. "Hello," he said. "Are you taking the freight?"

"Yes. I'm going to Montreal."

"We're going to ride together for a ways, then. I'm going as far as Latuque."

"Oh? How far is that?"

"About half-way to Montreal."

We waited until long after daylight before he spotted a freight slowly making its way toward us. With him leading the way, we found a boxcar and jumped in. We made our way to the very end of the car and sat down on our packsacks. The old man lighted a cigarette and asked if I was going home or just going for a visit.

"I'm going to visit some friends who own the Belmont Hotel," I said, and asked if he knew his way around Montreal.

"Oh, sure. I know Montreal like the palm of my hand. In fact, I stayed at the Belmont once when I had some money on me, but now I'm flat broke and I'm too old to find a job so I just bum up and down the railroad line." It was difficult to get any concrete information out of the old man because he would start to talk about one thing and then go on to a new subject without finishing the first one, but eventually I learned enough to help me find my way in Montreal.

"Don't worry about getting caught when you get to Latuque," he said. "Just get off when the freight slows down enough to jump, then walk for about two miles along the edge of the bush until you get to the water tank. Grab the same freight again there. But," he cautioned, "when you get to Harvey Junction, you have to watch out. There are a lot of bulls there and they sure like to grab you and throw you in the can for a week. Don't let any of them see you walking along the tracks with a packsack on your back or you'll wind up in jail. You'll be safe once you pass the station and get to the water tank; just make sure you take the freight heading south or you'll wind up in Quebec City."

He seemed to mumble and drift off into his own thoughts, then come back as if there had been no lapse in the conversation.

"It's the same when you get to Montreal," he continued. "Watch out for the bulls; there are a lot of them there, too. When you jump off, you'll find yourself in hobo jungle. Don't even jingle a silver coin in your pocket or they'll steal every cent you've got. Tell any of them that approach you that you are broke and hungry; that way they'll leave you alone."

He seemed exhausted after parting with all that information. Sitting on the floor with his back against the all, he went to sleep.

The freight rolled along at a good speed, stopping at what looked like logging camp sidings now and then to hook on a car, or to leave one behind.

Feeling hungry, I dug in my packsack for some bread and salted pork I had cooked before leaving the farm. The old man woke up and asked if I could spare him some food so I handed him the bread and butter and he made himself a couple of sandwiches. He ate one, put the other in his pocket, and went back to sleep.

When we came to a fairly big town I woke him up to ask what town it was. He looked out the door and said, "That's Latuque. I'm getting off here." He placed his packsack by the door and when the freight slowed down he said, "Goodbye," and jumped off.

I closed the door and waited in a corner for a long time before the train got going again. It felt good to be alone for a change; I'd had enough company to last me awhile. Now I could relax and think in peace about what to do next.

The freight had been rolling along at a fast clip for a long time and I was deep in thought when I was startled by the sound of the whistle blowing. Jumping to my feet, I looked out the door and saw that we were almost at Harvey Junction. I got hold of my packsack and was ready to jump, but the train didn't seem to be slowing down. I was getting panicky because there were people standing on the platform and I knew I had to make a move right away if I didn't want to get caught.

I ran to the other side of the car and pulled open the door. Throwing out my packsack, I jumped right behind it, landed on my feet, then stumbled and fell by the side of the tracks. Quickly I picked myself up, grabbed my packsack and ran for the nearby forest.

I walked into the forest until I was certain no one could see me from the railroad, then walked parallel to the tracks until I was a long way past the station. When I came to an open field, I saw the water tank ahead. There were only low shrubs growing in the field, with the same type of shrubs surrounding the water tank.

As I got closer to the tank I could see the remains of campfires and other spots where former freight riders had slept. It was a nice area, reminding me a bit of where my family used to go to pick blueberries. I sat down on the sandy ground to wait for the next freight.

A few minutes later two men came along, well dressed, with small, clean packsacks strapped to their backs. One had on a shiny wristwatch. They walked past without noticing me, settling down a few feet away. I could hear them talking about Montreal and I knew they, too, were waiting for the freight.

We had been waiting for about half an hour when one of the men walked past me to relieve himself a bit farther on. On his way back, he finally noticed me and was quite startled. He went back to his friend, said something in a very low voice, then they both got up, put on their packsacks and headed for the tracks. The train had pulled in and was taking on water.

I was about to follow them when I saw a man dressed in a blue uniform get up from where he had been hiding and yell to them, "Where do you think you're going? Stop where you are!"

The men stopped and the railroad cop handcuffed the one to the other and led them away. I was so scared I couldn't stop shaking, thinking that it could have been me in handcuffs, too, if I had followed them. I stayed hidden behind some low bushes near the railroad tracks and watched the three of them disappear as they crossed behind the caboose.

When they were safely out of sight I grabbed my packsack and ran from one clump of shrubs to the next until I saw an open boxcar. Making a dash for it, I threw my packsack in and jumped in myself. Not more than two minutes later the engineer blew a short whistle and we began to move.

I had been too frightened to notice at first, but both doors of the boxcar were open, which was good. If a cop showed up at one of the doors, I could escape from the other.

After awhile I began to relax and enjoy the ride. Looking out the door at the scenery, I could see we were going through some flat land covered with low shrubs. There weren't any tall trees, or even a house in sight. It was a completely deserted area.

Feeling sleepy, I went to a corner and sat down, but I knew I couldn't afford the luxury of a nap. The old hobo hadn't mentioned how long it would take to get to Montreal and I hadn't thought of asking. So I'd just have to keep watch, and listen for the whistle of the locomotive.

As hard as I tried to stay awake, I just couldn't and I was fast asleep when the whistle woke me up. Jumping to my feet, I grabbed my packsack and dragged it to the door. Hanging tightly to the door frame, I looked out, but I couldn't see anything that looked like a city coming up. I ran to the other door and looked out that side, too, but I still couldn't see any sign of life.

The freight was rolling fast on a straight stretch of tracks and before long I heard a long whistle and two short ones. Now I could see a maze of viaducts and overhead passes ahead, all seeming to intermingle with one another. There were old buildings, some with tall chimneys spewing smoke, and everything looked black and dirty.

The freight began to slow down and I thought of what the old hobo had said: he could jump off a freight while traveling at twenty miles per hour. The trick was to jump facing the direction the freight was traveling. He had fallen on his face once, but didn't get hurt.

The train wasn't slowing down that much and if it didn't stop soon, we would be right in the city. I was getting scared, but I kept my packsack in one hand and waited. Finally we began to slow down, but we must have been going at least twenty miles per hour when I threw out my packsack and jumped after it. I landed on my feet and found myself running almost as fast as the freight.

I had to run back at least five hundred feet to retrieve my packsack, then I jumped over the fence and into the shrubs. The old hobo was right, it was like a jungle, but not the one he meant. I could see that was farther ahead. The shrubs were so thick where I was I could barely make my way through them, being careful not to tear my clothes because some of the shrubs had long, sharp thorns. In spite of my care, my face got scratched a few times.

I finally got out of that jungle and saw a man a short distance ahead who seemed to be waiting for me. He was a funny-looking little man of about twenty-five, wearing a big smile that distorted his face even more than it already was. He had the deepest blue eyes I had ever seen, a big pug nose, and his cheeks were covered with freckles. He was about five foot two and wore a navy blue toque and a long, heavy, black overcoat that dragged on the ground. He reminded me of a little gnome I had read about in a storybook.

When I reached him, he asked, "Where are you from?"

"From the north and I'm starving. I just got off the freight."

He was very friendly. "I have a pot of barley soup on the fire. I just came to get some more wood for the night as it's going to be a cold one. Come on, I'll give you some soup."

I was sorry I had told him I was hungry, because I didn't know if he could spare the soup.

This, then, was the real hobo jungle. The ground was littered with cardboard boxes, planks, and concrete slabs. There were men–dirty men dressed in rags–standing near barrels with a fire burning inside. The air reeked with smoke and the smell of rotting garbage and soiled clothes. Even after spending five months on the trapline and sleeping in our clothes for all that time, my father and I never smelled as bad as that.

The little gnome showed me his home: a slab of concrete sidewalk supported by a concrete block at each end, with an old mattress for a bed. Hurriedly, he went to the fire and stirred his soup. I thanked him but said my uncle expected me that night and he'd have supper ready when I got there, if I could find his place.

He asked where my uncle lived and I told him, "The Belmont Hotel on Ste. Catherine Street."

"That's only a half a dozen blocks from here, so you're okay; you're almost there."

He was more than happy to help. "I can take you right to the door. It's less than a ten-minute walk from here." He grabbed my packsack and led the way.

After walking four short blocks, we came to Ste. Catherine Street. Stopping on the corner, he pointed: "You see that red neon sign there? That says The Belmont." He turned to go back, but before he could leave I dug in my pocket and handed him a dollar. He looked at it and smiled. "Thank you. You must be rich."

I walked slowly along the sidewalk opposite the hotel, keeping an alert eye open for the taxi. Seeing nothing of interest, I crossed over to the other side and walked quickly past the hotel, turning into what I thought was an alley, but was instead a parking area. I checked out the parked cars, but none of them were Rodger's. It was getting dark and I needed a place to wait, so I decided to stay in the parking lot since it was fairly secluded. I dropped my packsack and sat on a concrete block near the dead-end alley from where I could see the cars going by. At first the traffic was rather heavy, but after awhile there was only the odd car going by, along with the few pedestrians who walked past the parking lot.

By this time I was hungry so I gnawed on a piece of bologna and ate a wedge of cold bannock. My stomach full, I began to get sleepy and wished I could find some place to lie down.

Checking the street once more, I was suddenly wide awake. A man with Joe's distinctive stride was walking by. I could hardly believe my eyes, but I was almost positive it was Joe, although I had never seen him move that fast. Wherever he was going, he was in a hurry to get there. Standing up to get a better look, I could see that it was indeed Joe, but I sat right down again because I didn't want him to see me. No, I couldn't take a chance on that. The temptation to follow him was almost irresistible, but I stayed where I was, my eyes glued to the street, and less than half an hour later Joe came back carrying a brown paper bag under his arm. He'd gone somewhere to buy liquor.

After sitting in the parking lot for what seemed like an awfully long time, I decided to walk to the front of the hotel and look through the window. Standing on my toes to see inside, I noticed a big clock on the wall that told me it was a quarter to eleven. My eyes roamed around the lobby and I could see a white-haired man in his late sixties sitting behind the desk reading a newspaper.

Joe and Rodger were in that hotel and I had to get up the gumption to go in and rent a room, even if I didn't accomplish anything after that. But first, I returned to the parking lot and sat down to think of a likely story to tell the hotel clerk

Entering the lobby, I walked directly to the desk and asked if a man named Joe Martel had rented a room earlier in the day. The clerk looked in the register and said, "Yes, him and a Rodger Belcour rented a room this afternoon."

"Mr. Martel is my uncle," I told him. "I got a letter a few days ago from my aunt saying that Uncle Joe would be staying at this hotel for a few days and it would be nice if I could come and visit him. She knows I work not far away. So I thought I'd show up unexpectedly and give Uncle Joe a surprise. I'd sure appreciate it if you could give me a room next to his."

Looking at the keys in the pigeonholes, he said, "Sure, I'll give you 211; they're in 209."

I signed the register with a fake name, paid him a dollar fifty, and he handed me the key.

Packsack on my back, I slowly climbed the creaky stairs to the second floor, tiptoeing past 209. Quietly unlocking 211, I hurried inside, put down the packsack and surveyed my surroundings. It looked more like a room in a flophouse than a hotel. On each side of the room was an army-type cot covered with gray wool blankets. A bare light bulb hung in the middle of the ceiling. The plaster on the walls was cracked and in some places had fallen off, leaving the laths showing. On the outside wall was a small window, the curtains hanging at an odd angle because the rod had come partly off its hook.

It wasn't the sort of place one would willingly spend the night. My mother had told me about hotels like this–flophouses where the doors didn't lock and the rooms were full of bedbugs and lice. Gingerly, I sat down on the only safe place in the room: a wooden kitchen chair.

As clearly as if I were in the same room I could hear Joe and Rodger talking. Joe asked Rodger if he wanted another drink.

"No, I still have some in my glass," said Rodger. "All I want right now is a good, long night's sleep. I'm tired. That was a long drive and you were too drunk to help me fix the flat tire; I had to do it all by myself. You were so drunk you could barely stand up."

"We got here just the same, didn't we?" Joe replied. "You have just one more drink and you'll sleep like a log."

Restless, I got up and quietly walked around the room. I looked out the window and checked for a ledge, but there wasn't one, so I opened the door and looked down the hallway. There was a lighted sign at the far end that read, Fire Exit, and I knew that door would lead outside. If I were in a hurry, I could probably use that exit to escape.

My bed was next to the wall separating our two rooms. When I pulled it out a few inches I could see a big hole where the plaster had fallen off, revealing the laths of wood crisscrossing one another. Sitting on the floor with my back against the wall, I had no trouble hearing their conversation, loud and clear.

"What we should do tomorrow morning," said Rodger, "is split the money fifty-fifty, go to a bank and make a deposit. It's stupid to carry that much cash around with us."

Joe didn't agree. "We can split the money all right, but I'm not depositing my share anywhere. The best bank is my packsack–well, the kid's packsack, so to speak."

Rodger laughed. "I wonder how he felt when he woke up the next morning. It's too bad we had to do it that way but–there we go again–it was me had to do it. You leave all the dirty work for me. I even had to find a gold buyer for you. I did all the most important work on this job, so I've made up my mind. We're going to split the money in the morning and we'll each do whatever we want with it."

The whiskey was being consumed steadily and by this time Rodger could barely get the words out of his mouth. Joe began to sing and wanted Rodger to join him. "You sing all you want," said Rodger, "but I'm going to bed."

By listening to their conversation, I was sure the money was still in the packsack somewhere in their room. All I had to do was get in there and find it.

Joe was still singing in a much lower voice, garbling some of the words, when I got out my hunting knife and began cutting away some of the laths. Very quietly and slowly, I kept at it until I had a hole almost large enough to crawl through.

I heard a glass fall and break on the bare wooden floor, and it wasn't long before Joe was snoring.

Feeling safe now, I began to chip away at their side of the wall and soon had a hole large enough to see into their room. To my surprise, the packsack was under the bed, near the wall. I renewed the chipping with more vigor than ever until the hole was large enough to drag the small packsack through. Grabbing it, I pulled it into the room and placed it on the bed. There was a lot of money in it and I began counting my share—ten thousand four hundred and fifty dollars.

Moving quickly, I put the money at the bottom of my packsack, under all my clothing. Then, remembering the extra twenty Joe owed me, I grabbed one and put it in my pocket. As I was closing the packsack, I got an idea. I dug out that nice nugget I got at the Chesterville mine and put it in with their money where they were sure to find it. I wanted them to know it was me that had taken the money. We were even now, and it felt great.

Closing the packsack, I put it under their bed again and cleaned the floor of all the tell-tale plaster and chips. Then I strapped on my packsack and left the room, leaving the hotel by the fire escape so no one would see me. Once outside, I found myself on a small landing that led to a ladder and in just a few seconds I dropped down into a dark alley.

CHAPTER XII

The alley was so dark it was frightening, and the thought of having so much money on me didn't help. I looked all around me–as much as I could see–but the surroundings were strange and I didn't know which way to go.

All kinds of thoughts entered my mind, especially: what if a cop saw me and stated asking questions? I'd have to come up with some good answers. I thought of a few, but if he searched my packsack and found all that money, he would want to know where it came from and I'd have to tell the truth. The only solution was to find a fast and safe way of getting out of Montreal–the sooner, the better.

Walking toward the faint lights at the end of the alley, I finally came to a well-lighted street; after coming out of that darkness it was almost like daytime. Both sides of the street were deserted except for the occasional parked car. Since I didn't know where I was going, it didn't matter what direction I went so I just started walking, hoping to find someone who could direct me to the railroad station or a bus depot. After walking five or six blocks, I saw a taxi parked along the curb in the next block and hurried to get to it. The driver pulled out before I got there, but it had given me an idea: that might be the safest way for me to get out of the city. I could hire a taxi to take me to the next town, and from there I could take the train home. I was convinced my plan would work. Not only would it get me out of town quickly, but it ought to confuse anybody who tried to follow me.

I had stopped in the shadow of a store entrance to gather my thoughts when I spotted another taxi slowly driving in my direction. Stepping quickly to the curb, I waved and he stopped in front of me and got out. "Where would you like to go?" he asked.

Like an idiot, I didn't know what to say, so I said the first thing that came into my head: "The next big town north of here. I'm going north."

The driver scratched his head for a minute. "There are lots of town north of Montreal. If you were going anywhere near Maniwaki, I could take a chance and drive you as far as Ste.-Agathe."

My dad had been to Maniwaki and I had heard him talk about it a few times. I didn't waste any time. "Maniwaki; that's the place I want to go."

He opened the back door and I got in, throwing my packsack down on the seat beside me. Hungry now, I thought of all the food I had with me, but I was too embarrassed to get any out and eat it in the taxi.

After we had driven a few miles I asked the driver how far it was to Ste.-Agathe. "Over forty miles. It's more than twenty miles past my limit, but I'm willing to take that chance because I need the money to make a payment on my car this month. But I'm going to charge you five dollars extra for going past my limit. By the way," he added, "how about giving me a twenty now and the rest at the end of the trip?"

"How much will it cost for the entire trip?"

"Well, it'll cost you twenty, and for the extra five I'll let you out at another taxi stand so you don't have to walk around town to look for one."

I undid the safety pin from my shirt pocket, took out the hundred that had been hidden there, found two tens and a five and handed it all to him. After thanking me, he put the money in his side pocket and began whistling. He must have felt good about getting paid in advance because he whistled all the way to Ste.-Agathe.

After about an hour we got to Ste.-Agathe and a short time later the driver stopped in front of a taxi stand. Yelling to another driver who was fast asleep in his car, he asked, "Can you drive this young fell as far as you can? He's going to Maniwaki."

The driver, wide awake now, straightened up in his seat. "I can only take him as far as Riviere Rouge and drop him off at the halfway house. I got picked up last month for going over my limit and had to pay a five-hundred-dollar fine. I sure can't afford to get caught again."

Transferring to the new taxi, I handed my packsack to the driver and he put it in the trunk. When I got a closer look at him it occurred to me he may have lied about his age in order to get a driver's licence. He might have been twenty-one, but he didn't look any older than me. When he started the car I asked him what time it was. He looked at his shiny wristwatch and said, "It's a quarter to five."

When we got to the halfway house I paid him the eight-dollar fare. The house stood near the road, in total darkness, with no other buildings anywhere around. As hungry as I was, I would have made myself go in and order a big breakfast of pork and beans if it had been open.

Loading on my packsack, I asked the driver how far it was to Maniwaki. "Another forty miles or so," he said, turning the car around and driving off into the night.

It was going to be a gray day, with at least two more hours before daylight. I began to walk at a steady pace, but I was too hungry and sleepy to go very far. I decided to look for a suitable spot to take to the bushes where I could light a fire and have something to eat and a good, long sleep. I hadn't had a good night's sleep in the past forty-eight hours and I needed the rest. I had a long journey ahead of me and from here on I had to be very rational in planning my trip if I wanted to get home safely, without any incidents.

About three miles down the road there as a clearing in the forest and I saw a spot near a small stream where the ground was sandy. I walked a few hundred feet into the bush and stopped in an area where there was a lot of dry wood. Putting down my packsack, I built a big fire and mixed a batch of crepes, eating four large ones with brown sugar. Shortly after, I began to doze by the warmth of the fire. Shaking myself awake, I got up and made a bed, covered myself with two blankets, and soon I was fast asleep.

When I awoke, I felt very rested but I was freezing cold and hungry again. The sky was still gray and the daylight waning, so I guessed it was nearing evening. I fried some salted pork and boiled some thinly sliced potatoes in the frying pan and had a good meal.

At nightfall I got back on the road, walking at a pace that I could keep up over a long distance. I kept walking until daylight, stopping only once to eat a piece of bannock that was getting rather stale and dry.

I bedded down again a few hundred feet from the road, but I was wide awake long before it turned dark. Anxious to be on my way, I got back on the road that afternoon, with a fair amount of daylight left.

I hardly felt the weight of the load I was carrying. It felt so good to be free from the hassle of going to work at the mine, and to be out of the city and back in the wilderness where I knew what to expect and how to handle almost any situation. I was intoxicated with my freedom until I saw headlights nearly a mile behind me. Hurrying off the road, I hid behind some bushes and waited for the car to go by. I got scared right out of my mind when it went slowly by me and I could see Rodger at the wheel.

I didn't get back on the road, but kept walking in the bushes and at a much slower pace.

About three hours later I saw some lights in the distance Making sure I didn't make any noise, I kept going until I got closer and could see it was some kind of hunting lodge where they rent rooms and sell meals. I was a few hundred feet from the lodge when I heard a dog barking, so I retreated, crossing the road and walking on the other side.

The dog didn't make any more noise, even when I stood directly across from the lodge, from where I could see Rodger's car parked by the side entrance.

A change of plans was necessary. Obviously, it would no longer be safe for me to walk on the road; I'd have to stay in the bush until I reached Maniwaki. The rest of the night, until morning, was spent at the foot of a big balsam tree. Unable to build a fire for fear of being discovered, I was frozen stiff when I awoke in the afternoon.

Because I was running low on food, I had to settle for a very light meal before starting out again. But my spirits lifted when, through the ebbing light of early evening, I could see patches of cleared land farther ahead. There were small houses scattered here and there that had been built with boards. It looked much like the area I came from, where settlers cleared the land for farming.

Making a long detour through the bush, I kept going very cautiously until I came to a place where there had once been a sawmill. There was a huge pile of sawdust and an empty, abandoned building. This was far enough from any settlers, and from the town itself, that I would be safe so I decided to settle there for the night. There was a small lake nearby where I could get water to make a big pot of tea and I could build a fire to keep warm.

I sat by the fire for a long time, planning my next more. What was the best thing to do now? Joe and Rodger were looking for me and I had no idea how long they would keep looking.

I knew one thing: I would have to go to town first thing in the morning and buy some food before they got on the road. From here on I couldn't take the risk of using the highway to get to Maniwaki; I'd have to stick to the safety of the forest, and to do that I had to carry my food with me. Also, it could snow at any time, so I would have to buy a pair of snowshoes. I just couldn't afford to get caught without them.

As I sat by the fire making my plans, I began to think of the possibility of cutting through the forest again after leaving Maniwaki. The more I thought about it, the more I liked the idea. If I had to buy extra gear anyway, I should just continue my trip that way. It would shorten the distance by at least fifty miles.

My mind was made up. I would try to reach the Marquis River and come out at our old cabin.

The next morning I would not only purchase food and snowshoes, but I would also buy a rifle and an axe. Those were the only extras I would need to make the trip home through the forest. At the Marquis

River I could spend a few days resting before starting the next eighty miles home. It would be nice to see the old cabin again.

I stayed up late that evening, happy about having made up my mind. Once I got to the Marquis River I knew my way home, so there wouldn't be any problems. It would be a fun trip, one I would remember for a long time. I checked which direction north was and then, satisfied I had my bearings, dug myself into a deep hole in the warm sawdust and pulled up two blankets.

Early the next morning I built a big fire and had breakfast. The sky still looked gray and forbidding and a strong northern wind was blowing. It was freezing cold. Hiding my packsack in the bush, I started out for town, although I knew it was too early for the stores to be open. The town couldn't be very far away, so there was no rush, but I hurried along anyway, just to keep warm.

Two miles later, I saw the first farmhouse and a dog barked as I passed by. Farther on I came to the highway and turned left and it wasn't long before I could see the small town of Maniwaki. When I came to the general store I could see people inside, but the door was locked.

I walked around to the back of the store and sat on a sawhorse near a huge pile of logs, waiting for what seemed like a long time before the store opened.

"May I help you?" asked the young woman behind the counter.

I told her my dad and I were starting a trapline nearby and he had sent me to buy some supplies while he looked for a place to build a cabin. "I'll look around and if I need some help, I'll ask," I said.

The first thing I spotted was the rifle rack near the door. I picked up a 30-30 Winchester just like my dad's and asked the price.

"Forty-five dollars."

I set it aside and continued looking around, noticing a bin full of moccasins. I bought a pair of them, a pair of insoles, woolen mitts and a short-handled axe that would be easy to carry in the bush. Then I picked out a pair of showshoes, two boxes of shells and a supply of food.

There wasn't quite enough money in my shirt pocket so, trying to be inconspicuous, I dug into my hip pocket for the balance. The store owner put everything in a feed bag for me to carry back to the old sawmill.

By the time I got back it was too late in the day to start my long journey, so I decided to heat some water and wash my clothes. I found everything I needed around the old mill. While I had some water heated

I even had a sponge bath, ignoring the cold air which, at any rate, felt good on my skin.

I went to bed early and was up with the dawn. The sky was still gray, with the clouds hanging low overhead–a sure sign of snow. I gathered my belongings and started out.

The snow began to fall shortly after lunch and I was getting tired, so I didn't go very far that first day. I was packing a fairly heavy load–a lot heavier than I had anticipated. The snow stopped falling by late afternoon and the sky cleared, promising a cold night. I had walked about twelve miles when I came to a big balsam tree and decided to spend the night under its long, sweeping boughs. After a good supper of canned pork and beans, I snuggled comfortably on some boughs and went to sleep.

It was very annoying to be awakened by the howls of a large pack of wolves. It sounded like there may have been eight or ten at least and they carried on their mournful howling for what seemed like hours before I could get back to sleep.

I woke up a bit tired from lack of sleep and crawled out into the open to find about four inches of snow on the ground. The sky was a clear blue, a good day for walking. Hurriedly, I ate some breakfast and got on my way.

After I'd gone about two miles I came to a maze of wolf tracks–the spot where they had had their party. Looking around, I spotted a moose lying half hidden under the boughs of a tree. When I got closer, I could see he was still alive, with part of his hindquarters and flank torn open and eaten away. I loaded my rifle and finished him off, then opened him up and took out his liver.

To make sure I was going in the right direction to find the Marquis River, I'd peel the bark off the butt of a black spruce now and then; the dark side showed me where north was.

Late that afternoon I came to a river; the current was fast and it wasn't frozen yet. I walked along the banks for the rest of the afternoon before coming to where the water was frozen. As I inched my way across, I kept checking the thickness of the ice until I reached the other side where I made camp there for the night.

I sat by a roaring fire, eating my supper, not very happy with the progress I had made the past two days: a little more than thirty miles by my reckoning. I would have to do a lot better than that in the next few days. A bit discouraged, I took the money out of my packsack and counted it, looking at it for a long time before putting it back. Somehow, just seeing all that money again made me feel better.

The next morning I lightened my packsack by about twenty-five pounds by leaving behind all the canned food, some flour, potatoes (they had frozen by then), and both blankets. The blankets had proven too bulky to carry on top of my packsack and kept catching in the branches, slowing me down.

On the fourth day I came to a very large lake that I had never seen before. A strange feeling came over me. Had I wandered a long way off my path and maybe lost my direction? Was I lost? I built a fire near the shore and brewed a pot of tea. Sitting there for a long time, I tried to reorient myself.

My dad always said, "If you ever get lost, the best thing to do is just sit down and think things over. Eventually it will all come back to you and you'll get on the right track again."

I decided to detour the lake—to keep it on my right, thinking that if I had wandered away from the direction of the Marquis River, then by swerving to my left I could come out somewhere along the Mont Laurier highway. I was fairly sure the highway wasn't too far away.

About halfway around the lake, I changed my mind again. I crossed the last part of the lake and then veered to my right and kept going in that direction for the rest of the day, walking until long after dark.

I knew I had walked more than thirty miles that day and would be able to reach our old cabin before nightfall the next day. I felt very confident when I bedded down for the night. I was on the right track now; the terrain looked exactly the same as that which surrounded the Marquis River.

When I woke up it was still dark and I realized I had slept for only a few hours. I guess anxiety had set in. However, I felt very rested, so I got up and was on my way long before daylight. I walked much faster than when I had started out and kept going until I was too hungry to go any farther.

After lunch I was on my way again and had gone just a short distance when I spotted some fresh blazes on a tree. They had been made by a white man, I knew, because Indians didn't blaze trees. Walking closer to have a good look, I could see they were fresh. Looking ahead, through thick willows, I could see a bit of a trail so I began to follow it. The willows were loaded with fresh snow, bent over and almost blocking the trail, making it hard to follow. Even walking was difficult.

I kept watching for pieces of cut willows to make sure I was still on the trail, but when I came to a small stream I looked up, and less than a hundred feet away was a newly-built cabin.

Surprised and happy to have come upon someone's cabin, I was still looking at it when the door opened and out came my dad. He had heard the sound of twigs breaking and had seen me through the small window.

Dad busted out in a loud laugh. "My friend," he exclaimed, "how did you ever find me here and what are you doing, coming from that direction? Did you get lost?"

"No, I wasn't lost. I walked all the way from Maniwaki. I left there about five days ago."

"Well, come on in," he said. "You see that little stream in front of you? That's the head of the Ottawa River. Come on in," he repeated. "I've been expecting you. I knew you'd come and spend the winter with me. I just read my tea leaves this morning and I could see you on the trail in my cup."

I entered the cabin and threw my packsack on the floor. Dad began to prepare me a meal but I told him I had just had my lunch a couple of hours earlier. Then he sat on the small wooden bench by the table and I began to tell him all about my adventurous few months at the mine and of my freight ride to Montreal.

I got on my knees and began to unpack, piling my belongings on the table. Dad moved to the bed to make more room for me. When I came to the big stacks of money, I handed them to him, telling him there was ten thousand four hundred and fifty dollars in all.

Dad took the elastic bands off and threw the money in the air. It rained down on the bed like rice at a wedding. He looked at it for a moment, then flung himself on his back on top of all that money and lay with his hands crossed over his chest.

"My friend," he said, "we're rich. Yes sirree, we're rich. I'm going to go and pick up my traps in the morning. We won't need to trap any more. I'm going to leave them in the cabin here; you never know, some poor trapper might find this place and use them. You and me are going to head for home as soon as I have that done. We won't be doing any more trapping. No sirree. We're not going to do any more trapping. I am going to sell the farm in the spring and we are going to move to the Peace River district where the land is a lot easier to clear. I've always wanted to see that area. Yes sirree, we are going to move to Pouce Coupe."

Dad was silent for a while, then he said, "Of course, I hear there are a lot of beavers and muskrats in the Peace River district…."

I just smiled. Some things never change. And what's wrong with that?

AUTHOR'S NOTE

Although written as a work of fiction, most of the events in this story took place as described. The years spent in the forest with my father are as real to me today as if they happened yesterday. A time long gone, but never forgotten.

Susan Rice